Thomas Bernhard

THE LOSER

Thomas Bernhard was born in Holland in 1931 and grew up in Austria. He studied music at the Universität Mozarteum in Salzburg. In 1957 he began a second career as a playwright, poet, and novelist. The winner of the three most distinguished and coveted literary prizes awarded in Germany, he has become one of the most widely translated and admired writers of his generation. His novels published in English include *Gargoyles*, *The Lime Works*, *Correction*, *Concrete*, *Woodcutters*, and *Wittgenstein's Nephew*; a number of his plays have been produced off-Broadway, at the Guthrie Theater in Minneapolis, and at theaters in London and throughout Europe. The five segments of his memoir were published in one volume, *Gathering Evidence*, in 1985. Thomas Bernhard died in 1989.

THE LOSER

THE LOSER

THOMAS BERNHARD

Translated from the German by Jack Dawson

Afterword by Mark M. Anderson

Vintage International
Vintage Books
A Division of Random House, Inc.
New York

TRANSLATOR'S NOTE

For English-speaking readers approaching a novel by Thomas Bernhard for the first time, a word about his somewhat peculiar orthography and punctuation may be in order. Bernhard's sentences are very long, even for a German reader accustomed to extended, complex sentence constructions. Further, the logical transitions between clauses ("but," "although," "whereas") are often missing or contradictory, and the verb tenses are rarely in agreement. Bernhard's frequent and unpredictable underlining also defies conventional usage. Sometimes he italicizes the title of Bach's compositions, sometimes he treats them like a common noun. On the other hand, he often gives the names of restaurants, towns, pianos, and people an emphasis that conventional German and English orthography exclude. These and similar oddities have been rigorously maintained in the present translation as the reflection of Bernhard's characteristic voice.

J.D.

THE LOSER

Suicide calculated well in advance, I thought,
no spontaneous act of desperation.

Even Glenn Gould, our friend and the most important piano virtuoso of the century, only made it to the age of fifty-one, I thought to myself as I entered the inn.

Now of course he didn't kill himself like Wertheimer, but died, as they say, a *natural death*.

Four and a half months in New York and always the *Goldberg Variations* and the *Art of the Fugue*, four and a half months of *Klavierexerzitien,* as Glenn Gould always said only in German, I thought.

Exactly twenty-eight years ago we had lived in Leopoldskron and studied with Horowitz and we (at least Wertheimer and I, but of course not Glenn Gould) learned more from Horowitz during a completely rain-drenched summer than during eight previous years at the Mozarteum and the Vienna Academy. Horowitz rendered all our professors null and void. But these dreadful teachers had been necessary to understand Horowitz. For two and a half months it rained without stopping and we locked ourselves in our rooms in Leopoldskron and worked day and night, insomnia (Glenn Gould's) had become a necessary state for us, during the night we worked through what Horowitz had taught us the day before. We ate almost nothing and the whole time never had the backaches we habitually suffered from with our former teachers; with Horowitz the backaches disappeared because we were studying so intensely they couldn't appear. Once our course with Horowitz was over it was clear that Glenn was already a better piano player than Horowitz himself, and from that moment on Glenn was the most important piano virtuoso in the world for me, no matter how many piano players I heard from that moment on, none of them played like Glenn, even Rubinstein, whom I've always loved, wasn't better. Wertheimer and I were equally good, even Wertheimer always said, Glenn is the best, even if we didn't yet dare to say that he was *the best player of the century*. When Glenn went back to Canada we had actually lost *our Canadian friend*, we didn't think we'd ever see him again, he was so possessed by his art that we had to assume he couldn't continue in that state for very long and would soon die. But two years after we'd studied together under Horowitz Glenn came to the Salzburg Festival to play the Goldberg Variations, which two years previously he had practiced with us day and night at the Mozarteum and had rehearsed again and again. After the concert the papers wrote that *no pianist* had ever played the Goldberg Variations so artistically, that is, after his Salzburg concert they wrote what we had already claimed and known two years previously.

We had agreed to meet with Glenn after his concert at the *Ganshof* in Maxglan, an old inn I particularly like. We drank water and didn't say a thing. At this reunion I told Glenn straight off that Wertheimer (who had come to Salzburg from Vienna) and I hadn't believed for a minute we would ever see him, Glenn, again, we were constantly plagued by the thought that Glenn would destroy himself after returning to Canada from Salzburg, destroy himself with his *music obsession*, with his *piano radicalism*. I actually said the words *piano radicalism* to him. *My piano radicalism*, Glenn always said afterward, and I know that he always used this expression, even in Canada and in America. Even then, almost thirty years before his death, Glenn never loved any composer more than Bach, Handel was his second favorite, he despised Beethoven, even Mozart was no longer the composer I loved above all others when *he* spoke about him, I thought, as I entered the inn. Glenn never played a single note without humming, I thought, no other piano player ever had that habit. He spoke of his lung disease as if it were his second art. That we had the same illness at the same time and then always came down with it again, I thought, and in the end even Wertheimer got *our* illness. But Glenn didn't die from this lung disease, I thought. He was killed by the impasse he had *played* himself into for almost forty years, I thought. He never gave up the piano, I thought, of course not, whereas Wertheimer and I gave up the piano because we never attained the inhuman state that

Glenn attained, who by the way never escaped this inhuman state, who didn't even want to escape this inhuman state. Wertheimer had his *Bösendorfer* grand piano auctioned off in the Dorotheum, I gave away my *Steinway* one day to the nine-year-old daughter of a schoolteacher in Neukirchen near Altmünster so as not to be tortured by it any longer. The teacher's child ruined my Steinway in the shortest period imaginable, I wasn't pained by this fact, on the contrary, I observed this cretinous destruction of my piano with perverse pleasure. Wertheimer, as he always said, had gone into the *human sciences*, I had begun my *deterioration process*. Without my music, which from one day to the next I could no longer tolerate, I deteriorated, without *practical* music, *theoretical* music from the very first moment had only a catastrophic effect on me. From one moment to the next I hated my piano, my own, couldn't bear to hear myself play again; I no longer wanted to *paw* at my instrument. So one day I visited the teacher to announce my gift to him, my Steinway, I'd heard his daughter was musically gifted, I said to him and announced the delivery of my Steinway to his house. I'd convinced myself *just in time* that personally I wasn't suited for a virtuoso career, I said to the teacher, since I always wanted only *the highest* in everything I had to separate myself from my instrument, for with it I would surely not reach the highest, as I had suddenly realized, and therefore it was only logical that I should put my piano at the disposal of his gifted daughter, I wouldn't open the cover of my piano even once, I said to the astonished teacher, a rather primitive man who was married to an even more primitive woman, also from Neukirchen near Altmünster. Naturally I'll take care of the delivery costs! I said to the teacher, whom I've known well since I was a child, just as I've known his simplicity, not to say stupidity. The teacher accepted my gift *immediately*, I thought as I entered the inn. I hadn't believed in his daughter's talent for a minute; the children of country schoolteachers are always touted as having talent, above all musical talent, but in truth they're not talented in anything, all these children are always completely without talent and even if one of them can blow into a flute or pluck a zither or bang on a piano, that's no proof of talent. I knew I was giving up my expensive instrument to an absolutely worthless individual and precisely for that reason I had it delivered to the teacher. The teacher's daughter took my instrument, one of the very best, one of the rarest and therefore most sought after and therefore also most expensive pianos in the world, and in the shortest period imaginable destroyed it, rendered it worthless. But of course it was precisely this destruction process of my beloved Steinway that I had *wanted*. Wertheimer went into the human sciences, as he always used to say, I entered my deterioration process, and in bringing my instrument to the teacher's house I had initiated this deterioration process in the best possible manner. Wertheimer continued to play the piano years after I had given my Steinway to the teacher's daughter because for years he thought himself capable of becoming a piano virtuoso. By the way he played a thousand times better than the majority of our piano virtuosos with public careers, but in the end he wasn't satisfied with being (in the best of cases!) another piano virtuoso like all the others in Europe, and he gave it all up, went into the human sciences. I myself played, I believe, better than Wertheimer, but I would never have been able to play as well as Glenn and for that reason (hence for the same reason as Wertheimer!) I gave up the piano from one moment to the next. I would have had to play better than Glenn, but that wasn't possible, was out of the question, and therefore I gave up playing the piano. I woke up one day in April, I no longer know which one, and said to myself, *no more piano*. And I never touched the instrument again. I went immediately to the schoolteacher and announced the delivery of my piano. I will now devote myself to philosophical matters, I thought as I walked to the teacher's house, even though of course I didn't have the faintest idea what these philosophical matters might be. I am absolutely not a piano virtuoso, I said to myself, I am not an interpreter, I am not a reproducing artist. No artist at all. The depravity of my idea had appealed to me immediately. The whole time on my way to the teacher's I kept on saying these three words: *Absolutely no artist! Absolutely no artist! Absolutely no artist!* If I hadn't met Glenn Gould, I probably wouldn't have given up the piano and I would have become a piano virtuoso and perhaps even one of the best piano virtuosos in the world, I thought in the inn. When we meet the very best, we have to give up, I thought. Strangely enough I met Glenn on Monk's Mountain, my childhood mountain. Of course I had seen him previously at the Mozarteum but hadn't exchanged a word with him before our meeting on Monk's Mountain, which is also called Suicide Mountain, since it is especially suited for suicide and every week at least three or four people throw themselves off it into the void. The prospective suicides ride the elevator inside the mountain to the top, take a few steps and hurl themselves down to the city below. Their smashed remains on the street have always fascinated me and I personally (like Wertheimer by the way!) have often climbed or ridden the elevator to the top of Monk's Mountain with the intention of hurling myself into the void, but I didn't throw myself off (nor did Wertheimer!). Several times I had already prepared myself to jump (like Wertheimer!) but didn't jump, like Wertheimer. I turned back. Of course many more people have turned back than have actually jumped, I thought. I met Glenn on Monk's Mountain at the so-called *Judge's Peak*, where one has the best view of Germany. I spoke first, I said, *both of us are studying with Horowitz. Yes*, he answered. We looked down at the German plain and Glenn immediately began setting forth his ideas about the *Art of the Fugue*. I've encountered a highly intelligent man of science, I thought to myself. He had a Rockefeller scholarship, he said. Otherwise his father was a rich man. Hides, furs, he said, speaking German better than our fellow students from the Austrian provinces. Luckily Salzburg is here and not four kilometers farther down in Germany, he said, I wouldn't have gone to Germany. From the first moment ours was a *spiritual* friendship. The majority of even the most famous piano players haven't a clue about their art, he said. But it's like that in all the arts, I said, just like that in painting, in literature, I said, even philosophers are ignorant of philosophy. Most artists are ignorant of their art. They have a dilettante's notion of art, remain stuck all their lives in dilettantism, even the most famous artists in the world. We understood each other immediately, we were, I have to say it, attracted from the first moment by our differences, which actually were completely opposite in our of course identical *conception of art*. Just a few days after this encounter on Monk's Mountain we ran into Wertheimer. Glenn, Wertheimer and I, after living separately for the first two weeks, all in completely unacceptable quarters in the Old Town, finally rented a house in Leopoldskron for the duration of our course with Horowitz where we could do what we pleased. In town everything had a debilitating effect on us, the air was unbreathable, the people were intolerable, the damp walls had contaminated us and our instruments. In fact we could only have continued Horowitz's course by moving out of Salzburg, which at bottom is the sworn enemy of all art and culture, a cretinous provincial dump with stupid people and cold walls where everything without exception is eventually made cretinous. It was our salvation to pack our worldly goods and move out to Leopoldskron, which at that time was still a green meadow where cows grazed and hundreds of thousands of birds made their home. The town of Salzburg itself, which today is freshly painted even in the darkest corners and is even more disgusting than it was twenty-eight years ago, was and is antagonistic to everything of value in a human being, and in time destroys it; we figured that out at once and took off for Leopoldskron. The people in Salzburg have always been dreadful, like their climate, and when I enter the town today not only is my judgment confirmed, everything is even more dreadful. But to study with Horowitz precisely in this town, the sworn enemy of culture and art, was surely the greatest advantage. We study better in hostile surroundings than in hospitable ones, a student is always well advised to choose a hostile place of study rather than a hospitable one, for the hospitable place will rob him of the better part of his concentration for his studies, the hostile place on the other hand will allow him total concentration, since he *must* concentrate on his studies to avoid despairing, and to that extent one can absolutely recommend Salzburg, probably like all other so-called beautiful towns, as a place of study, of course only to someone with a strong character, a weak character will inevitably be destroyed in the briefest time. Glenn was charmed *by the magic* of this town for three days, then he suddenly saw that its magic, as they call it, was rotten, that basically its beauty is disgusting and that the people living in this disgusting beauty are vulgar. The climate in the lower Alps makes for emotionally disturbed people who fall victim to cretinism at a very early age and who *in time* become *malevolent*, I said. Whoever lives here knows this if he's honest, and whoever comes here realizes it after a short while and must get away before it's too late, before he becomes just like these cretinous inhabitants, these emotionally disturbed Salzburgers who kill off everything that isn't yet like them with their cretinism. At first he thought how nice it must be to grow up here, but two, three days after his arrival he already realized what a nightmare it was to be born and raised here, to become an adult here. This climate and these walls kill off all sensitivity, he said. I couldn't have said it better. In Leopoldskron we were safe from the town's boorishness, I thought as I entered the inn. Basically it wasn't only Horowitz who taught me to play the piano to its absolute capacity, it was my daily contact with Glenn Gould during the Horowitz course, I thought. It was the two of them who made music possible for me, gave me a concept of music, I thought. My last teacher before Horowitz had been Wührer, one of those teachers who suffocate a pupil with their own mediocrity, not to mention the teachers who finished their degrees earlier and who all have brilliant careers, as they say, performing at every moment in world cities and occupying highly paid chairs at our famous music conservatories, but they're nothing but piano-playing executioners without the faintest understanding of the concept of music, I thought. These music teachers are playing and sitting everywhere and ruining thousands and hundreds of thousands of music students, as if it were their life's mission to suffocate the exceptional talent of our musical youth before it's developed. Nowhere does such irresponsibility reign as it does in our music conservatories, which lately have taken to calling themselves music *universities*, I thought. Out of twenty thousand music teachers only one is ideal, I thought. Glenn, had he devoted himself to it, would have been such a teacher. Glenn had, like Horowitz, the ideal sensibility and the ideal intelligence for teaching, for communicating his art. Every year tens of thousands of music students tread the path of music conservatory cretinism and are destroyed by unqualified teachers, I thought. Become famous in some instances and still haven't understood a thing, I thought as I entered the inn. Become Gulda or Brendel and still are nothing. Become Gilels and still are nothing. Even Wertheimer, if he hadn't met Glenn, would have become one of our most important piano virtuosos, I thought, he wouldn't have had to misuse the human sciences, so to speak, as I misused philosophy, for just as I had misused philosophy or rather philosophical matters for decades, so Wertheimer had misused the so-called human sciences to the very end. He wouldn't have written all those slips of paper, I thought, just as I wouldn't have completed my manuscripts, those crimes against the intellect, as I thought while entering the inn. We begin as piano virtuosos and then start rummaging about and foraging in the human sciences and philosophy and finally go to seed. Because we didn't reach the absolute limit and go beyond this limit, I thought, because we gave up in the face of a genius in our field. But if I'm honest I could never have become a piano virtuoso, because at bottom I never wanted to be a piano virtuoso, because I always had the greatest misgivings about it and misused my virtuosity at the piano in my deterioration process, indeed I always felt from the beginning that piano players were ridiculous; seduced by my thoroughly remarkable talent at the piano, I drilled it into my piano playing and then, after one and a half decades of torture, chased it back out again, abruptly, unscrupulously. It's not my way to sacrifice my existence to sentimentality. I burst into laughter and had the piano brought to the teacher's house and amused myself for days with my own laughter about the piano delivery, that's the truth, I laughed at my piano virtuoso career, which went up in smoke in a single moment. And probably this piano virtuoso career that I had suddenly tossed aside was a necessary part of my deterioration process, I thought while entering the inn. We try out all possible avenues and then abandon them, abruptly throw decades of work in the garbage can. Wertheimer was always slower, never as decisive in his decisions as I, he tossed his piano virtuosity in the garbage can years after me and, unlike me, he didn't get over it, never did, again and again I heard him bellyaching that he never should have stopped playing the piano, he should have continued, *I* was partly responsible, was always his model in important issues, in existential decisions, as he once put it, I thought as I entered the inn. Taking Horowitz's course was as deadly for me as it was for Wertheimer, for Glenn however it was a stroke of genius. Wertheimer and I, as far as our piano virtuosity and in fact music generally were concerned, weren't killed by Horowitz but by Glenn, I thought. Glenn destroyed our piano virtuosity at a time when we still firmly believed in our piano virtuosity. For years after our Horowitz course we believed in our virtuosity, whereas it was dead from the moment we met Glenn. Who knows, if I hadn't gone to Horowitz, that is if I had listened to my teacher Wührer, whether I wouldn't be a piano virtuoso today, one of those famous ones, as I thought, who shuttle back and forth the whole year between Buenos Aires and Vienna with their art. And Wertheimer as well. Immediately I quashed that idea, for I detested virtuosity and its attendant features from the very beginning, I detested above all appearing before the populace, I absolutely detested the applause, I couldn't stand it, for years I didn't know, is it the bad air in concert halls or the applause I can't stand, or both, until I realized that I couldn't stand *virtuosity* per se and especially not piano virtuosity. For I absolutely detested the public and everything that had to do with this public and therefore I detested the virtuoso (and virtuosos) personally as well. And Glenn himself played in public only for two or three years, then he couldn't stand it anymore and stayed home and became, in his house in America, the best and most important piano player of them all. When we visited him for the last time twelve years ago he had already given up public concerts ten years before. In the meantime he had become the most sharp-witted fool around. He had reached the summit of his art and it was only a matter of the shortest time before a stroke would lay him low. At the time Wertheimer also felt that Glenn had only the shortest amount of time left to live, he'll have a stroke, he said to me. We spent two and a half weeks in Glenn's house, which he had equipped with his own recording *studio*. As he had during our Horowitz course in Salzburg, he played the piano pretty much night and day. For years, for an entire decade. I've given thirty-four concerts in two years, that's enough for my whole life, Glenn had said. Wertheimer and I played Brahms with Glenn from two in the afternoon till one in the morning. Glenn had stationed three bodyguards around his house to keep his fans off his back. At first we hadn't wanted to bother him and planned to stay only one night, but we wound up staying two and a half weeks, and both Wertheimer and I realized once again how right we were to have given up our piano virtuosity. *My dear loser*, Glenn greeted

Wertheimer, with his Canadian-American cold-bloodedness he always called him *the loser*, he called me quite dryly *the philosopher*, which didn't bother me. Wertheimer, *the loser*, was for Glenn always busy losing, constantly losing out, whereas Glenn noticed I had the word *philosopher* in my mouth at all times and probably with sickening regularity, and so quite naturally we were for him *the loser* and *the philosopher*, I said to myself upon entering the inn. The *loser* and the *philosopher* went to America to see Glenn the piano virtuoso again, for no other reason. And to spend four and a half months in New York. For the most part together with Glenn. He didn't miss Europe, Glenn said right off as he greeted us. Europe was out of the question. He had *barricaded* himself in his house. For life. All our lives the three of us have shared the desire to barricade ourselves from the world. All three of us were born barricade fanatics. But Glenn had carried his barricade fanaticism furthest. In New York we lived next to the Taft Hotel, there wasn't a better location for our purposes. Glenn had a Steinway set up in one of the back rooms at the Taft and played there every day for eight to ten hours, often at night as well. He didn't go a day without playing the piano. Wertheimer and I loved New York right from the start. It's the most beautiful city in the world and it also has the best air, we repeated again and again, nowhere in the world have we breathed better air. Glenn confirmed what we sensed: New York is the only city in the world where a thinking person can breathe freely the minute he sets foot in it. Glenn visited us every three weeks, showing us the hidden corners of Manhattan. The Mozarteum was a bad school, I thought as I entered the inn, on the other hand for us it was the best because it opened our eyes. All schools are bad and the one we attend is always the worst if it doesn't open our eyes. What lousy teachers we had to put up with, teachers who screwed up our heads. Art destroyers all of them, art liquidators, culture assassins, murderers of students. Horowitz was an exception, Markevitch, Végh, I thought. But a Horowitz doesn't make a first-rate conservatory by himself, I thought. The plodders ruled the building, which was more famous than any other in the world and still is today; if I say I studied at the Mozarteum people get all weepy-eyed. Wertheimer, like Glenn, was the son of wealthy parents, not merely well-to-do. I myself was also free of all material worries. It's always an advantage to have friends from the same social sphere and the same economic background, I thought as I entered the inn. Since basically we had no financial worries we could devote ourselves exclusively to our studies, carry them out in the most radical way possible, we also had nothing else on our minds, we simply had to keep removing the roadblocks in our way, our professors in all their mediocrity and hideousness. The Mozarteum is world famous even today, but it is absolutely the worst music conservatory imaginable, I thought. But if I hadn't gone to the Mozarteum I would never have met

Wertheimer and Glenn, I thought, my friends for
life. Today I can no longer say how I came to
music, everyone in my family was unmusical,
against art, had never hated anything more than
art and culture their entire lives, but that probably
was what motivated me to fall in love one day with
the piano I had initially hated, and trade in my
family's old Ehrbar for a truly wonderful Steinway
in order to show up my hated family, to set out
in the direction they had abhorred from the first.
It wasn't art, or music, or the piano, but opposition to my family, I thought. I had hated playing
the Ehrbar, my parents had forced it on me as they
had on all the children in our family, the Ehrbar
was their artistic center and with it they had
slogged their way to the last pieces by Brahms and
Reger. I had *hated* this family artistic center but
loved the Steinway, which I had blackmailed my
father into having delivered from Paris under the
most frightful circumstances. I had to enroll in the
Mozarteum to show them, I didn't have the faintest idea about music and playing the piano had
never exactly been one of my passions, but I used
it as a means to an end against my parents and my
entire family, I exploited it against them and I
began to *master* it against them, better from day
to day, with increasing virtuosity from year to
year. I enrolled in the Mozarteum against them, I
thought in the inn. Our Ehrbar stood in the so-
called music room and was the artistic center where
they showed off on Saturday afternoons. They
avoided the Steinway, people stayed away, the

Steinway put an end to the Ehrbar epoch. From the day I played the Steinway the artistic center in my parents' house was kaput. The Steinway, I thought while standing in the inn and looking about, was aimed against my family. I enrolled in the Mozarteum to take my revenge on them, for no other reason, to punish them for their crimes against me. Now they had an artist for a son, an abominable species from their point of view. And I misused the Mozarteum against them, put all its means into play against them. Had I taken over their brickyards and played their old Ehrbar all my life they would have been satisfied, but I cut myself off from them by setting up the Steinway in the music room, which cost a fortune and did indeed have to be delivered from Paris to our house. At first I had insisted on the Steinway, then, as was only proper for the Steinway, on the Mozarteum. I brooked, as I must now say, no opposition. I had decided to become an artist overnight and demanded everything. I caught them unawares, I thought as I looked around in the inn. The Steinway was my barricade against them, against their world, against family and world cretinism. I was not a born piano virtuoso, as Glenn was, perhaps even Wertheimer, although I can't claim that with absolute certainty, but I quite simply forced myself to become one, talked and played myself into it, I must say, with absolute ruthlessness in their regard. With the Steinway I could suddenly appear on stage against them. I made myself into an artist out of desperation, into the most obvious sort available, a piano virtuoso, if possible into a world-class piano virtuoso, the hated Ehrbar in our music room had given me the idea and I developed this idea as a weapon against them, exploiting it to the highest and absolutely highest degree of perfection against them. Glenn's case was no different, nor was Wertheimer's, who had studied art and therefore music only to insult his father, as I know, I thought in the inn. The fact that I'm studying the piano is a catastrophe for my father, Wertheimer said to me. Glenn said it even more radically: they hate me and my piano. I say Bach and they're ready to throw up, said Glenn. He was already world famous and his parents still hadn't changed their point of view. But whereas he stayed true to his principles and in the last and final analysis was able, if only two or three years before his death, to convince them of his genius, Wertheimer and I proved our parents right by failing to become virtuosos, failing indeed very quickly, *in the most shameful manner*, as I often was privileged to hear my father say. But my failure to become a piano virtuoso never bothered me, unlike Wertheimer, who suffered right to the end of his life for having given up, given himself over to the human sciences, which until the end he could never define, just as even today I still don't know what philosophy, what philosophical matters generally, might be. Glenn is the victor, we are the failures, I thought in the inn. Glenn put an end to his existence at the only true moment, I thought. And he didn't finish it off himself, that is by his own hand, as did Wertheimer, who had no other choice, who had to hang himself, I thought. Just as one could predict Glenn's end well in advance, so one could predict Wertheimer's end long in advance, I thought. Glenn is said to have suffered a fatal stroke in the middle of the Goldberg Variations. Wertheimer couldn't take Glenn's death. After Glenn's death he was ashamed to still be alive, to have outlived the genius so to speak, that fact martyred him his entire last year, as I know. Two days after reading in the newspaper that Glenn had died we received telegrams from Glenn's father announcing his son's death. The second he sat down at the piano he sank into himself, I thought, he looked like an animal then, on closer inspection like a cripple, on even closer inspection like the sharp-witted, beautiful man that he was. He, Glenn, had learned German from his maternal grandmother, which he spoke fluently, as I've already indicated. With his pronunciation he put our German and Austrian fellow students to shame, since they spoke a completely barbaric German and speak this completely barbaric German all their lives because they have no sense for their own language. But how can an artist have no feeling for his native language? Glenn often asked. Year in, year out he wore the same kind of pants, if not the same pants, his step was light, or as my father would have said, noble. He loved things with sharp contours, detested approximation. One of his favorite words was *self-discipline*, he said it over and over, even in class with Horowitz, as I remember. He loved best to run out on the street shortly after midnight, or at least out of the house, I'd already noticed that in Leopoldskron. We must always fill our lungs with a good dose of fresh air, he said, otherwise we won't go forward, we'll be paralyzed in our efforts to reach the highest. He was the most ruthless person toward himself. He never allowed himself to be imprecise. He spoke only after thinking his way through a problem. He abhorred people who said things that hadn't been thought through, thus he abhorred almost all mankind. And more than twenty years ago he finally withdrew from this abhorred mankind. He was the only world-famous piano virtuoso who abhorred his public and also actually withdrew definitively from this abhorred public. He didn't need them. He bought himself a house in the woods and settled into this house and went about perfecting himself. He and Bach lived in this house in America until his death. He was a fanatic about order. Everything in his house was order. When I first walked through the door with Wertheimer, I had to think of his *concept of self-discipline*. After we were inside he didn't ask us, for example, if we were thirsty but sat down at his Steinway and played for us those passages from the Goldberg Variations that he had played in Leopoldskron the day before his departure for Canada. His technique was as perfect as it was then. At that moment I realized that no one else in the world could play like that. He sank into himself and started in. Started low and played upwards, so to speak, not like all the others, who played from the top down. That was his secret. For years I tormented myself with the question whether it was right to visit him in America. A pitiful question. At first Wertheimer didn't want to, I finally talked him into it. Wertheimer's sister was against her brother visiting the world-famous Glenn Gould, whom she considered dangerous for him. Wertheimer finally prevailed over his sister and came with me to America and to Glenn. Over and over I kept telling myself, this is our last chance to see Glenn. I actually was expecting his death and I had absolutely wanted to see him again, hear him play, I thought as I stood in the inn and inhaled the inn's fetid aroma, which was all too familiar. I knew Wankham. I always stayed in this inn when I was in Wankham, when I visited Wertheimer, since I couldn't stay with Wertheimer, he couldn't tolerate overnight guests. I looked for the innkeeper, but everything was still. Wertheimer hated having guests stay overnight, abhorred them. Guests in general, of any kind, he received them and paid them compliments, they were barely in the door before they were out again, not that he would have complimented me out the door, I knew him too well for that, but after a few hours he preferred me to disappear rather than stay and spend the night. I've never spent the night at his house, it never would have occurred to me, I thought, keeping a sharp lookout for the innkeeper. Glenn was a big-city person, like me incidentally, like Wertheimer, at bottom we loved everything about big cities and hated the country, which however we exploited to the hilt (as we did the city, incidentally, in its own way). Wertheimer and Glenn had finally moved to the country because of their sick lungs, Wertheimer more reluctantly than Glenn, Glenn on principle, since he finally could no longer put up with people in general, Wertheimer because of his continuous coughing fits in the city and because his internist told him he had no chance of surviving in the big city. For over two decades Wertheimer found refuge with his sister at the Kohlmarkt, in one of the biggest and most luxurious apartments in Vienna. But finally his sister married a so-called industrialist from Switzerland and moved in with her husband in Zizers bei Chur. Of all places Switzerland and of all people a chemical-plant owner, as Wertheimer expressed it to me. A horrendous match. She left me in the lurch, blubbered Wertheimer over and over. In his suddenly empty apartment he appeared paralyzed, after his sister moved out he would sit for days in a chair without moving, then start running from room to room like the proverbial chicken, back and forth, until he finally holed himself up in his father's hunting lodge in Traich. After his parents' death he nonetheless lived with his sister and tyrannized this sister for twenty years, as I know, for years he kept her from having any contact with men and with society in general, umbrellaed her off so to speak, chained her to herself. But she broke loose and ditched him along with the old, rickety furniture they had inherited together. How could she do this to me, he said to me, I thought. I've done everything for her, sacrificed myself for her, and now she's left me behind, just ditched me, runs after this nouveau-riche character in Switzerland, Wertheimer said, I thought in the inn. In Chur of all places, that ghastly region where the Catholic church literally stinks to high heaven. Zizers, what a godawful name for a town! he exploded, asking me if I'd ever been in Zizers, and I recalled having passed through Zizers several times on my way to St. Moritz, I thought. Provincial cretins, cloisters and chemical plants, nothing else, he said. He worked himself up several times to the claim that he had given up his piano virtuosity for love of his sister, *I called it quits because of her*, sacrificed my career, he said, gave away everything that had meant anything to me. This was how he tried to lie his way out of his own desperation, I thought. His apartment at the Kohlmarkt extended over three floors and was stuffed full of every conceivable artwork, which always oppressed me when I visited my friend. He himself confessed to hating these artworks, his sister hoarded them, he hated them, couldn't care less about them, blamed his entire misfortune on his sister, who had ditched him for a Swiss megalomaniac. He once told me quite seriously that he had dreamed of growing old with his sister in the Kohlmarkt apartment, *I'll grow old with her here, in these rooms*, he once told me. Things turned out differently, his sister slipped away from him, turned her back on him, perhaps at the very last possible moment, I thought. He didn't leave the apartment until months after his sister's marriage, transforming himself as it were from a sitter into a walker. In his best moments he would walk from the Kohlmarkt to the Twentieth District and from there to the Twenty-first through Leopoldstadt and back to the First, strolling for hours back and forth in the First until he couldn't walk any farther. In the country he was virtually paralyzed. There he would barely walk a few steps to the woods. The country bores me, he said again and again. Glenn is right to call me the *pavement walker*, said Wertheimer, *I only walk on pavement, I don't walk in the country, it's awfully boring and I stay in the hut*. What he called a hut was the hunting lodge he inherited from his parents and which had fourteen rooms. The fact is that in this hunting lodge he would get dressed as if he were going on a fifty- or sixty-kilometer hike—leather hiking boots, thick woolen garments, a felt cap on his head. But he would step outside only to discover that he didn't want to go hiking and would get undressed and sit down in the room downstairs and stare at the wall in front of him. My internist says I don't have a chance in the city, he said, but here I have absolutely no chance. I hate the country. On the other hand I want to follow my internist's instructions so that I'll have nothing to reproach myself for. But to go hiking or even to go for a walk in the country—that I can't do. It makes no sense to me at all, I can't commit this sort of nonsense, I won't commit the crime of this nonsense. I regularly get dressed, he said, and walk out the door and turn around and get undressed again, no matter what the season, it's always the same. At least nobody sees my craziness, he said, I thought in the inn. Like Glenn Wertheimer couldn't tolerate anybody around him. Thus in time he became impossible. But I too, I thought, standing in the inn, would never have been able to live in the country, that's why I live in Madrid and wouldn't even consider leaving Madrid, this most magnificent of all cities where I have everything the world has to offer. Those who live in the country get idiotic in time, without noticing it, for a while they think it's original and good for their health, but life in the country is not original at all, for anyone who wasn't born in and for the country it shows a lack of taste and is only harmful to their health. The people who go walking in the country walk right into their own funeral in the country and at the very least they lead a grotesque existence which leads them first into idiocy, then into an absurd death. To recommend country life to a city person so that he can stay alive is a dirty internist's trick, I thought. All these people who leave the city for the country so they can live longer and healthier lives are only horrible specimens of human beings, I thought. But in the end Wertheimer was not just the victim of his internist but even more the victim of his conviction that his sister lived only to serve him. He actually said several times that his sister was born for him, to stay with him, to protect him so to speak. No one has disappointed me like my sister! he once exclaimed, I thought. He grew fatally accustomed to his sister, I thought. On the day his sister left him he swore to her his eternal hatred and drew all the curtains in the Kohlmarkt apartment, never to open them again. Still he managed to keep his oath for fourteen days, on the fourteenth day he opened the curtains in the Kohlmarkt apartment and raced down to the street, half crazed and starved for food and people. But the loser collapsed on the Graben, as I know. He was brought back to his apartment only because a relative fortunately happened to be passing by at that instant, otherwise they probably would've carted him off to the mental ward at Steinhof, for he had the look of a wild man. Glenn wasn't the most difficult person among us, Wertheimer was. Glenn was strong, Wertheimer was our weakest. Glenn wasn't crazy, as people have always claimed and still claim, but Wertheimer was, as I claim. For twenty years he was able to chain his sister to him, with thousands, yes, hundreds of thousands of chains, then she broke loose from him and, as I believe, even married well, as they say. The already rich sister found herself a *stinking* rich Swiss husband. He could no longer tolerate the word sister or the word Chur, Wertheimer told me the last time I saw him. She didn't even send me a card, he said, I thought in the inn, looking around. She stole away from him in the night and left everything lying in the apartment, she didn't take a single thing with her, he said over and over. Although she promised she'd never leave me, never, he said, I thought. On top of that my sister *converted,* as he expressed himself, she is deeply Catholic, hopelessly Catholic, he said. But that's how these deeply religious, deeply Catholic converts are, he said, they're not afraid of anything, not even of the most heinous crime, they abandon their own brother and throw themselves in the arms of some dubious upstart, who has come into money unscrupulously and completely by accident, as Wertheimer said during my last visit, I thought. I can see him in front of me, hear his voice with the utmost clarity, those chopped sentences he always used and which fitted him to a T. *Our loser is a fanatic,* Glenn once said, *he's practically choking on self-pity all the time,* I can still see Glenn saying this, hear him saying it, we were on Monk's Mountain, at the so-called Judge's Peak, where I often went with Glenn but without Wertheimer when Wertheimer wanted to be by himself, without us, for whatever reason, very often in a huff. I always called him *the offended one.* After his sister moved out he withdrew to Traich with increasingly frequent regularity; because I hate Traich I go to Traich, as he said. The Kohlmarkt apartment started gathering dust because he wouldn't let anyone in in his absence. In Traich he often spent the whole day inside, had one of his woodsmen bring him a pot of milk, butter, bread, some smoked sausage. And would read his philosophers, Schopenhauer, Kant, Spinoza. In Traich he also kept the curtains drawn most of the time. Once I thought I'll buy myself another Bösendorfer, he said, but then I gave up the idea, that would be madness. By the way, I haven't touched the piano for the last fifteen years, he said, I thought in the inn, uncertain whether I should call out or not. It was the greatest folly to believe I could be an artist, lead an artist's existence. But I couldn't just flee right into the human sciences, I had to take this detour through art, he said. Do you think I could have become a great piano player? he asked me, naturally without waiting for an answer and laughing a dreadful *Never!* from deep inside. You yes, he said, but not me. You had what it takes, he said, I could see that, you played a few bars and I realized it, you yes, but not me. And with Glenn it was clear from the very start that he was a genius. Our American-Canadian genius. We both failed for the opposite reasons, Wertheimer said, I thought. I had nothing to prove, only everything to lose, he said, I thought. Our wealth was probably our undoing, he said, but then immediately: Glenn's wealth didn't kill him, it allowed him to exploit his genius. Yes, if only we hadn't run into Glenn, Wertheimer said. If only the name Horowitz had meant nothing to us. If only we had never even gone to Salzburg! he said. We caught up with death in that city by studying with Horowitz and meeting Glenn. Our friend meant our death. Of course we were better than all the others who studied with Horowitz, but Glenn was better than Horowitz himself, Wertheimer said, I can still hear him, I thought. On the other hand, he said, we're still alive, he isn't. So many in his circle had already died, he said, so many relatives, friends, acquaintances, none of these deaths ever shocked him, but Glenn's death dealt him a *deadly* blow, he pronounced *deadly* with extraordinary precision. We don't have to be with a person in order to feel bound to him as to no other, he said. Glenn's death had hit him *very hard*, he said, I thought while standing in the inn. Although one could have predicted this death more certainly than any other, that goes without saying, so he said. Nonetheless we still can't grasp it, we can't comprehend, can't grasp it. Glenn had had the greatest affection for the word and the concept of loser, I remember exactly how the word loser came to him on the Sigmund Haffnergasse. We look at people and see only cripples, Glenn once said to us, physical or mental or mental *and* physical, there are no others, I thought. The longer we look at someone, the more crippled he appears to us, because he is as crippled as we are unwilling to admit but as he actually is. The world is full of cripples. We go out on the street and meet only cripples. We invite someone into our house and we have a cripple for a guest, so Glenn said, I thought. I have actually noticed the same thing over and over and have only been able to confirm Glenn's point. Wertheimer, Glenn, myself, all cripples, I thought. Friendship, artistry! I thought, my God, what madness! I'm the survivor! Now I'm alone, I thought, since, to tell the truth, I only had two people in my life who gave it any meaning: Glenn and Wertheimer. Now Glenn and Wertheimer are dead and I have to come to terms with this fact. The inn struck me as rather shabby, like all inns in this region everything in it was dirty and the air, as they say, was so thick you could cut it with a knife. Everything about it was unappetizing. I could have long since called for the innkeeper, I knew her personally, but I didn't call. Wertheimer is reported to have slept with the innkeeper several times, naturally in her inn, not in his hunting lodge, I thought. At bottom Glenn played only the *Goldberg Variations* and the *Art of the Fugue*, even when he was playing other pieces, such as by Brahms and Mozart, or Schönberg and Webern; he held the latter two in the highest regard, but he placed Schönberg above Webern, not the other way around, as people claim. Wertheimer invited Glenn to Traich several times, but Glenn never returned to Europe after his concert at the Salzburg Festival. We didn't correspond either, for the few cards we sent each other in all those years can't be called a correspondence. Glenn regularly sent us his records and we thanked him for them, that was all. Basically we were bound by the unsentimental nature of our friendship, even Wertheimer was completely unsentimental, although the contrary seemed to be true. When he blubbered it wasn't sentimentality but self-interest, calculation. The idea of wanting to see Wertheimer's hunting lodge after his death suddenly struck me as absurd, I smacked my forehead, although without actually doing it. But my way of doing things is not at all sentimental, I thought while looking about the inn. At first I only wanted to visit the Kohlmarkt apartment in Vienna, then I decided to take the train to Traich in order to contemplate, one last time, the hunting lodge where Wertheimer spent the last two years, as I know, in the most awful circumstances. After his sister's marriage he had trouble staying in Vienna for three months, went wandering through the city, as I can imagine, spewing insults against his sister until he simply had to get out of Vienna, to hide himself in Traich. The last card he sent to Madrid had horrified me. His handwriting was the handwriting of an old man, one couldn't help noticing signs of madness in that card, of disconnected thoughts. But I had no intention of going to Austria, in my apartment in the Calle del Prado I had become too absorbed by my work *About Glenn Gould*, under no circumstances would I have interrupted this work, for then I would have botched it and I didn't want to risk that, so I didn't answer Wertheimer's card, which struck me as curious even as I was reading it. Wertheimer got the idea of flying to America to attend Glenn's funeral, I however refused, and he wouldn't fly alone. It took me three days after Wertheimer hanged himself to figure out that, like Glenn, he had just turned fifty-one. When we cross the threshold of our fiftieth year we see ourselves as base and spineless, I thought, the question is how long we can stand this condition. Lots of people kill themselves in their fifty-first year, I thought. Lots in their fifty-second, but more in their fifty-first. It doesn't matter whether they kill themselves in their fifty-first year or whether they die, as people say, a natural death, it doesn't matter whether they die like Glenn or whether they die like Werthei-mer. The reason is that they're often ashamed of having reached the limit that a fifty-year-old crosses when he puts his fiftieth year behind him. For fifty years are absolutely enough, I thought. We become contemptible when we go past fifty and are still living, continue our existence. We're border-crossing weaklings, I thought, who have made ourselves twice as pitiful by putting fifty years behind us. Now I'm the shameless one, I thought. I envied the dead. For a moment I hated them for their superiority. I considered it a lapse of judgment on my part to have traveled to Traich out of simple curiosity, the cheapest of all motives, while standing in the inn, disgusted by the inn, I disgusted myself most of all. And who knows, I thought, whether someone in the hunting lodge will even let me in, without a doubt the new own-ers are already there, as I know, for Wertheimer always described his relatives to me in such a way that I had to assume they hated me as much as they did him and that they considered me now, probably rightly, as the most ill-mannered of busy-bodies, I thought. I should have flown back to Madrid and never undertaken this completely use-less trip to Traich, I thought. I've got a lot of nerve, I thought. I suddenly felt like a grave-robber with my plan to look at the hunting lodge and enter every room in the hunting lodge, leaving no stone unturned and developing my own theories about it. I'm an awful person, hideous, revolting, I thought when I wanted to call the innkeeper but in the last moment didn't call her, all at once I was afraid she could come too early, that is appear too early for my purposes, disturb my thinking, wipe out the thoughts I'd suddenly had here, these Glenn- and Wertheimer-digressions which I had suddenly indulged in. I actually had planned and still plan to look over the writings that Wertheimer may have left behind. Wertheimer often spoke of writings he had been working on over the years. A lot of nonsense, as Wertheimer put it, but he was also arrogant, which led me to assume that this nonsense might be rather valuable, would at least contain Wertheimerian thoughts worth preserving, collecting, saving, ordering, I thought, and already I could see an entire stack of notebooks (and notes) containing more or less mathematical, philosophical observations. But his heirs won't fork over these notebooks (and notes), all these writings (and notes), I thought. They're not even going to let me in the hunting lodge. They're going to ask who I am and as soon as I tell them who I am they'll slam the door in my face. My reputation is so abominable they will slam their doors shut and lock them, I thought. This crazy idea of visiting the hunting lodge had already occurred to me in Madrid. It's possible that Wertheimer never told anyone but me about his writings (and notes), I thought, and tucked them away somewhere, so I owe it to him to dig out these notebooks and writings (and notes) and preserve them, no matter how difficult it proves to be. Glenn actually left nothing behind, Glenn didn't keep any kind of written record, I thought, Wertheimer on the contrary never stopped writing, for years, for decades. Above all I'll find this or that interesting observation about Glenn, I thought, at least something about the three of us, about our student years, about our teachers, about our development and about the development of the entire world, I thought as I stood in the inn and looked out the kitchen window, behind which however I could see nothing, for the windowpanes were black with filth. They cook in this filthy kitchen, I thought, from this filthy kitchen they bring out the food to the customers in the restaurant, I thought. Austrian inns are all filthy and unappetizing, I thought, one can barely get a clean tablecloth in one of these inns, never mind cloth napkins, which in Switzerland for instance are quite standard. Even the tiniest inn in Switzerland is clean and appetizing, even our finest Austrian hotels are filthy and unappetizing. And talk about the rooms! I thought. Often they just iron over sheets that have already been slept in, and it's not uncommon to find clumps of hair in the sink from the previous guest. Austrian inns have always turned my stomach, I thought. The plates aren't clean and upon closer inspection the silverware is almost always dirty. But Wertheimer often ate in these inns, at least once a day I want to see people, he said, even if it's just this decrepit, down-and-out, filthy innkeeper. So I go from one cage to the next, Wertheimer once said, from the Kohlmarkt apartment to Traich and then back again, he said, I thought. From the catastrophic big-city cage into the catastrophic forest cage. Now I hide myself here, now there, now in the Kohlmarkt perversity, now in the country-forest perversity. I slip out of one and back into the other. For life. But this procedure has become such a habit that I can't imagine doing anything else, he said. Glenn locked himself in his North American cage, I in my Upper Austrian one, Wertheimer said, I thought. He with his megalomania, I with my desperation. All three with our desperation, he said, I thought. I told Glenn about our hunting lodge, Wertheimer said, I'm convinced that that's what gave him the idea of building his own house in the woods, *his studio, his desperation machine*, Wertheimer once said, I thought. What a stroke of lunacy, to build myself a house with a recording studio in the middle of the woods, cut off from all human contact, miles away from everything, only a lunatic does something like that for himself, a candidate for the mental ward, said Wertheimer. I didn't have to build my desperation studio, I already had one in Traich. I inherited it from my father, who managed to stay here alone for years, was less delicate than I, less of a complainer, less pitiful, less absurd than I, Wertheimer once said. We have an ideal sister for our needs and she leaves us at exactly the wrong moment, completely unscrupulously, Wertheimer said.

Goes off to Switzerland where everything's going to pot, Switzerland is the most spineless country in Europe, he said, in Switzerland I've always had the feeling that I was in a whorehouse, he said. Everything whorish, the cities and the country, he said. St. Moritz, Saas Fee, Gstaad, all brothels, not to mention Zurich, Basel, world brothels, Wertheimer said on several occasions, world brothels, nothing but world brothels. This gloomy city Chur where the archbishop still says Good morning and Good night! he exploded. That's where my sister runs off to, runs away from me, her cruel brother, the destroyer of her life and being! Wertheimer said, I thought. To Zizers, where the Catholic church stinks to high heaven! Glenn's death has hit me very hard, I once heard him say clearly, while I stood in the restaurant, still in the same spot, I'd merely put my bag on the floor. Wertheimer had to commit suicide, I told myself, he had no future left. He'd used himself up, had run out of existence coupons. It's completely like him to have slept with the innkeeper in her inn, I thought, I looked up at the ceiling in the restaurant, reflecting that the two of them had probably joined bodies right above the restaurant, in the innkeeper's bed. The superaesthete in that filthy bed, I thought. Mr. Refinement, who always claimed he could live only with Schopenhauer, Kant, Spinoza, sleeping with the innkeeper from Wankham at more or less regular intervals underneath her cheap feather bed. At first I had to laugh out loud, then it turned my stomach.

No one had even heard my laughter. The inn-keeper remained out of sight. As I watched the dining room got dirtier and dirtier, the whole inn more and more questionable. But I had no other choice, *this* was and is the only inn in the area. Glenn, I thought, never played Chopin. Refused all the invitations, all the highest fees. He always talked people out of the idea that he was an un-happy person, he claimed he was *the happiest, the most blessed by happiness. Music / obsession / ambition / Glenn,* I had once noted in my first Madrid notebook. Those people in the Puerta del Sol that I described to Glenn in nineteen sixty-three after discovering *Hardy.* Description of a bullfight, Retiro Park speculations, I thought, that Glenn never acknowledged. Wertheimer often in-vited Glenn to Traich, the hunting lodge would surely be to his liking, Wertheimer thought, Glenn had never accepted the invitation, not even Werth-eimer was a hunting-lodge person, never mind Glenn Gould. Horowitz was never the mathe-matician that Glenn Gould was. *Was.* We say *he is,* then suddenly *he was,* this terrible *was,* I thought. Wertheimer would lecture at me when I was working on, for example, Schönberg, Glenn never would. He couldn't accept that someone knew more than he did, couldn't tolerate someone explaining something he didn't know about. Em-barrassed by his ignorance, I thought, standing in the inn and waiting for the innkeeper. On the other hand Wertheimer was the reader, not Glenn, not I, I didn't read a great deal and when I did it was always the same thing, the same books by the same authors, the same philosophers over and over as if they were always completely new. I had developed the art of perceiving the same thing over and over as something new, developed it to a high, absurdly high skill, neither Wertheimer nor Glenn had that skill. Glenn read almost nothing, he avoided literature, which was just like him. Only what really serves my own purposes, he once said, my art. He had all of Bach in his head, the same with Handel, a good deal of Mozart, all of Bartók as well, he could sit down and *interpret* for hours, that was his word for it, naturally without a mistake and brilliantly, *inglenniously*, as Wertheimer used to say. Basically I realized from the moment I met Glenn on Monk's Mountain that he was one of the most extraordinary people I had ever met in my life, I thought. The physiognomist in me isn't wrong. Years later the world confirmed my judgment, but this only pained me, like everything confirmed by the newspapers. We exist, we don't have any other choice, Glenn once said. It's total nonsense what we have to go through, even he, I thought. Even Wertheimer's death could have been predicted, I thought. Curiously Wertheimer always maintained that *I* would commit suicide, hang myself in the woods, *in your beloved Retiro Park*, he once said, I thought. He never forgave me for having just got up and left for Madrid, without saying a word to anyone, abandoning everything. He'd grown used to my walking through Vienna with him, for years, a whole decade, of course they were *his* walks, not mine, I thought. He always walked faster than me, I had trouble keeping up with him although *he* was the sick one, not I, precisely because *he* was the sick one he always walked ahead of me, I thought, left me behind as soon as we started out. *The loser* is one of Glenn Gould's brilliant inventions, I thought, Glenn just *saw through* Wertheimer the moment they met, he *completely saw through* everyone he met for the first time. Wertheimer got up at five in the morning, I got up at five-thirty, Glenn never before nine-thirty because he went to bed around four in the morning, not to sleep, said Glenn, but *to let the sound of my exhaustion die out.* Kill myself, I thought, now that Glenn is dead, that Wertheimer has committed suicide, as I looked around the restaurant. Glenn was always afraid of the dampness of Austrian restaurants, he feared death would claim him in these Austrian restaurants, where the air hardly circulates or not at all. Actually death claims many people in our restaurants, the innkeepers refuse to open the windows, not even in summer, and so the moisture seeps into the walls for eternity. And everywhere this gaudy new tastelessness, I thought, the complete proletarianization of even our most beautiful inns, I thought, continues unabated. No word has turned my stomach more than the word *socialism* when I think what people have done to this term. Everywhere this dog-do socialism spouted by our dog-do socialists who exploit the people with their socialism, eventually dragging it down to their own dog-do level. Today everywhere we look we see this *deadly dog-do-level socialism*, we smell it, it's penetrated everything. I know the rooms in this inn, I thought, they're deadly. The thought that I had come to Wankham merely to see Wertheimer's hunting lodge struck me at that moment as base. On the other hand, I told myself immediately, I owe it to Wertheimer, I repeated precisely this sentence, I owe it to Wertheimer, I said to myself out loud. One lie followed another. Curiosity, which has always been my most prominent character trait, had taken a firm grip on me. Perhaps the heirs have already moved everything out of the hunting lodge, I thought, changed it from top to bottom, heirs have an unscrupulous way of taking over that we can barely imagine. Clear out everything within hours of the deceased's final breath, as they say, cart it all away and won't let anyone in the door. No one ever cast a more damaging light on his relatives than Wertheimer, *described them into the dirt*. Hated his father, mother, sister, reproached them all with his unhappiness. That he had to continue existing, constantly reminding them that they had thrown him up into that awful existence machine so that he would be spewed out below, a mangled pulp. His mother threw her child into this existence machine, all his life his father kept this existence machine running, which accurately hacked his son to pieces. Parents know very well that they perpetuate their own unhappiness in their children, they go about it cruelly by having children and throwing them into the existence machine, he said, I thought, contemplating the restaurant. I first saw Wertheimer in the Nussdorferstrasse, in front of the Markthalle. He should have become a businessman like his father, but in fact he didn't even become a musician as he, Wertheimer, wanted but *was destroyed by the so-called human sciences,* as Wertheimer said. We run away from one thing into the other and destroy ourselves in the process, he said. We just simply go away until we have given up, so he said. Preference for cemeteries, like me, I thought, entire days spent in the cemeteries in Döbling and in Neustift am Wald, I thought. His lifelong yearning to be alone, I thought, is mine too. Wertheimer was no traveler like me. Was no passionate address-switcher. Once with his parents in Egypt, that was all. Whereas I exploited every opportunity to travel, no matter where, broke loose the first time to Venice for ten days with my grandfather's medical bag and one hundred and fifty schillings, visiting the Accademia by day and attending performances at La Fenice by night. *Tancredi* for the first time in *La Fenice*, I thought, my first desire *to make a go* at music. Wertheimer was always and only the loser. No one pounded the streets of Vienna like he did, coming and going in all directions again and again until he was totally exhausted. Diversion maneuvers, I thought. He wore out tremendous quantities of shoes. *Shoe fetishist* were words that Glenn once said to Wertheimer, I think he had hundreds of shoes in his Kohlmarkt apartment, and that was also a way he drove his sister to the brink of madness. He revered, indeed loved, his sister, I thought, and in time drove her crazy. In the nick of time she escaped his clutches by going to Zizers bei Chur, broke off all contact, ditched him. He left her clothes exactly the way she had kept them in her wardrobes. Didn't touch any of her things. Basically I *misused* my sister *as a page turner*, he once said, I thought. No one could turn pages like her, I taught her how in my ruthless manner, he once said, in the beginning she couldn't even read music. *My brilliant page turner*, he once said, I thought. He had degraded his sister into a page turner, in the long run she couldn't put up with it. His *she'll never find a husband* turned out to be a horrible mistake, I thought. Wertheimer had built a top-security prison for his sister, totally escapeproof, but she got away, in the dead of night, as they say. That had made Wertheimer terribly ashamed. Sitting in his armchair he became obsessed with the idea of killing himself, as he said, I thought, pondered over the proper method for days at a time, but then didn't do it. Glenn's death already made the thought of suicide a permanent frame of mind for him, his sister's escape strengthened this permanent frame of mind, as he related. Glenn's death drove home his own failure with furious clarity. As for his sister, it was her base, vicious nature to have abandoned him in a crisis situation for a thoroughly low-life character from Switzerland who wore tasteless raincoats with pointy lapels and Bally shoes with brass buckles,

as Wertheimer said, I thought. I should never have
let her go to that awful internist Horch (her doctor!), he said, for that's where she met that Swiss.
Doctors are in cahoots with chemical-plant owners, he said, I thought. *Never should have let her
go*, he said about his *forty-six-year-old* sister, I
thought. The forty-six-year-old had to ask his permission to go out, I thought, had to account for
every one of her outings. At first he, Wertheimer,
believed that the Swiss, whom he'd sized up as a
ruthlessly self-interested person, had married her
for her money, but then it turned out that he was
much richer than the two of them put together,
that is, *loaded*, Swiss rich, which is a good deal
richer than Austrian rich, as he put it. The father
of this person (the Swiss), said Wertheimer, had
been one of the directors of the Leu Bank in Zurich, just imagine, Wertheimer said, the son owns
one of the biggest chemical plants in the world!
His first wife lost her life in mysterious circumstances, no one knows what happened. My sister
as the second wife of some upstart, so Wertheimer,
I thought. Once he sat for eight hours in the ice-
cold St. Stephen's Cathedral and stared at the altar,
the beadle showed him the door to St. Stephen's
with the words: *Sir we're closing*. As he went out
he slipped the beadle a hundred-schilling bill, a
short-circuit operation, as Wertheimer put it. I
wanted to sit in St. Stephen's till I fell over dead,
he said. But I couldn't manage it, not even by
totally concentrating on this wish. It wasn't possible for me to be totally concentrated, and our

desires are realized only when we are totally concentrated. From early childhood he had experienced the wish to die, to commit suicide, as they
say, but never was totally concentrated. He could
never come to terms with being born into a world
that basically repulsed him in every detail from the
very beginning. He grew older and thought that
his wish to die would suddenly no longer be there,
but this wish grew more intense from year to year,
without ever becoming totally intense and concentrated. My constant curiosity got in the way
of my suicide, so he said, I thought. We never
forgive our fathers for having sired us, nor our
mothers for having brought us into the world, he
said, nor our sisters for continuing to *be* witnesses
to our unhappiness. To exist means nothing other
than we despair, he said. When I get up I'm re-
volted by myself and everything I have to do.
When I go to bed I have no other wish than to
die, never to wake up, but then I wake up again
and the awful process repeats itself, finally repeats
itself for fifty years, he said. To think that for fifty
years we don't wish for anything other than to be
dead and are still alive and can't change it because
we are thoroughly *in*consistent, so he said. Because we are wretched, vile creatures. No *musical
ability!* he cried out, *no life ability!* We're so arrogant that we think we're studying music whereas
we're not even capable of living, not even capable
of existing, for we don't exist, we get existed, so
he once said in the Währingerstrasse after we had
hiked through the Brigittenau to the point of com-

plete exhaustion for four and a half hours. Once we used to spend half the night in the *Koralle*, he said, now we don't even go to the *Kolosseum*! he said, *how everything has become absolutely unfavorable*. We think we have a friend and in time see we don't have a friend at all, since we have absolutely no one, that's the truth, so he said. He clung to his Bösendorfer and still everything had turned out to be a mistake, an awful mistake. Glenn had the good fortune of collapsing at his Steinway in the middle of the *Goldberg Variations*. He claimed he'd been trying to collapse for years, without success. Went several times with his sister to the so-called Promenade in the Prater to improve her health, he said, so that she could get some fresh air, but she didn't appreciate these outings, *why only the Prater Promenade and not the Burgenland, why only the Prater Promenade and not Kreuzenstein or Retz*, she was never satisfied, I did everything for her, she could buy every dress she wanted, he said. I pampered her, he said. At the height of being pampered, he said, she took off to Zizers bei Chur, to that awful place. They all run off to Switzerland when they're short of ideas, he said, I thought. But Switzerland turns into a deadly prison for all of them, little by little they choke on Switzerland in Switzerland, as my sister will choke on Switzerland, he could see it, Zizers will kill her, her Swiss husband will kill her, Switzerland will kill her, so he said, I thought. Zizers of all places, that perverse creation of a place name, so he said, I thought. It may have been our parents' plan, he said, my sister and I together for life, our parents' calculation. But this parental plan, this parental calculation didn't work out. We'll have a son, my parents may have thought, and then a sister, and the two of them will live together till death do them part, caring for one another, destroying one another, that may have been my parents' idea, their devilish idea, so he said. Parents make a plan, but naturally this plan doesn't work out, so he said. My sister didn't keep to the plan, she's the stronger one, so he said, I've always been the weak one, absolutely the weak link, so Wertheimer. He could barely catch his breath going uphill and still outraced me. He couldn't climb stairs and still got to the fourth floor faster than me, it was all a suicide attempt, I thought now while observing the restaurant, a futile attempt to escape life's clutches. Once he traveled to Passau with his sister because his father had convinced him that Passau was a beautiful town, a restful town, a remarkable town, but the minute they arrived in Passau they saw that Passau was one of the ugliest towns imaginable, a town over-eagerly imitating Salzburg, a town bursting with helpless and ugly and repulsively gauche ambition, which has the perverse arrogance to call itself Three River City. They took only a few steps in this Three River City before they turned around and, because the next train to Vienna didn't leave for hours, took a taxi back to Vienna. After their experience in Passau they renounced all travel plans for years, I thought. In later years, when his sister expressed a desire to travel, Wertheimer merely said to her: *remember Passau!* thereby nipping any travel debate in the bud. A desk from the age of Joseph II now stood where his auctioned Bösendorfer grand piano had been, I thought. But we don't always have to be studying something, I thought, it's perfectly enough merely to think, to do nothing but think and give our thoughts free rein. To give in to our philosophical worldview, simply submit to our philosophical worldview, but that's the hardest thing, I thought. Wertheimer wasn't up to such a feat when he had the Bösendorfer auctioned off, not even later, unlike me, I was up to it, I thought. This capacity also allowed me to vanish from Austria one day with just a small travel bag, at first to Portugal, then to Spain, and take up residence in the Calle del Prado, right next to *Sotheby's.* Suddenly, overnight so to speak, I had become a *philosophical worldview artist.* This sudden verbal invention of mine made me laugh out loud. I took a few steps toward the kitchen window although I'd already realized I couldn't look through the kitchen window because, as already mentioned, it's covered with filth from top to bottom. Austrian kitchen windows are all totally filthy and we can't look through them and naturally it's to our greatest advantage, I thought, not to be able to look through them because then we find ourselves staring into the mouth of catastrophe, into the chaos of Austrian kitchen filth. So I reversed the few steps I had taken to the kitchen window and remained where I had been

standing the whole time. Glenn died at the perfect
moment, I thought, but Wertheimer didn't commit suicide at the perfect moment, whoever commits suicide never commits suicide at the perfect
moment, whereas a so-called natural death always
occurs at the perfect moment. Wertheimer had
wanted to compete with Glenn, I thought, to show
his sister, to *pay her back* for everything by hanging himself only a hundred steps from her house
in Zizers. He bought himself a train ticket for
Zizers bei Chur and went to Zizers and hanged
himself a hundred steps in front of his sister's
house. For several days they couldn't identify the
body. It took four or five days after finding the
body until a hospital official in Chur was struck
by the name *Wertheimer,* he connected the name
Wertheimer with the wife of the chemical-plant
owner, whom he knew previously as Frau Wertheimer, and, puzzled, inquired in Zizers about a
connection between the suicide victim Wertheimer
lying in his morgue and the wife of the chemical-
plant owner in Zizers. Wertheimer's sister, who
hadn't even known that someone had hanged himself a hundred steps from her front door, drove
straight to the morgue in Chur and identified the
body, as they say. Wertheimer's calculation
worked perfectly: he thrust his sister into a lifelong
guilt complex through the means and place of his
suicide, I thought. That calculation is just like
Wertheimer, I thought. But in doing so he made
himself ridiculous, I thought. He had already left
Traich with the intention of hanging himself

from a tree a hundred steps from his sister's house, I thought. Suicide calculated well in advance, I thought, no spontaneous act of desperation. I wouldn't have left Madrid to go to his funeral in Chur, I thought, but since I was already in Vienna it was natural to go to Chur. And from Chur to Traich. But now I was seriously wondering whether it wouldn't have been better to go to Vienna directly after Chur and not stop in Traich, at the moment it wasn't clear to me what I was looking for here apart from catering to a distinctly cheap sort of curiosity, since I had talked myself into the necessity of my being here, pretended it was necessary, faked it. I didn't tell Wertheimer's sister that I intended to go to Traich, and I wasn't thinking of it in Chur either, it was in the train that I first had the idea of getting out in Attnang-Puchheim and going back to Traich, spending the night in Wankham, as of course I had been used to doing from my previous visits to Traich, I thought. I've always thought, one day I'll go to Wertheimer's funeral, of course I never knew when, only that it would happen, even though I never voiced this thought, above all not in Wertheimer's presence, whereas he, Wertheimer, very often told me that *he* would go *to my* funeral one day, that's what I was thinking about while waiting for the innkeeper. And I had been certain that Wertheimer would kill himself one day for all these reasons, which were constantly in the front of my mind. Glenn's death, as it turned out, was not the crucial factor, his sister had to leave him, but

Glenn's death had been the beginning of the end, the triggering moment being his sister's marriage with the Swiss. Wertheimer had tried to save himself by walking through Vienna without ever stopping, but the attempt failed, rescue was out of the question, visits to his beloved blue-collar districts in the Twentieth and Twenty-first districts, above all Brigittenau, above all Kaisermühlen, the Prater with its indecencies, the Zirkusgasse, the Schüttelstrasse, the Radetzkystrasse, etc., all pointless. For months he had criss-crossed Vienna, day and night, to the point of collapse. It was no use. Even the hunting lodge in Traich, which he initially saw as a lifesaver, turned out to be a miscalculation; as I happen to know, he first locked himself into the hunting lodge for three weeks, then went to the woodsmen and burdened them with his problem. But simple people don't understand complicated ones and thrust the latter back on themselves, more ruthlessly than any others, I thought. The biggest mistake is to think that one can be rescued by so-called simple people. A person goes to them in an extremely needy condition and begs desperately to be rescued and they thrust this person even more deeply into his own despair. And how are they supposed to save the extravagant one in his extravagance, I thought. Wertheimer had no other choice but to kill himself after his sister left him, I thought. He wanted to publish a book, but it never came to that, for he kept changing his manuscript, changing it so often and to such an extent that nothing was left of the manuscript, for the change in his manuscript was nothing other than the complete deletion of the manuscript, of which finally nothing remained except the title, *The Loser*. From now on I have only the title, he said to me, it's better that way. I don't know if I have the energy to write another book, I don't think so, he said, if *The Loser* had ever been published I would have had to kill myself. On the other hand he was a note person, filled thousands, tens of thousands of paper slips with his handwriting and piled these notes in the Kohlmarkt apartment exactly as he did in the hunting lodge in Traich. Perhaps it is actually his notes that interest you and that caused you to get out in Attnang-Puchheim, I thought. Or only a procrastination maneuver, since you loathe Vienna. Thousands of his notes set end to end, I thought, and published under the title *The Loser*. Nonsense. I guessed that he'd destroyed all these notes in Traich and Vienna. *Don't leave any traces behind* was of course one of his sayings. If a friend dies we nail him to his own sayings, his comments, kill him with his own weapons. On the one hand he lives on in what he said to us (and to others) all his life, on the other we kill him with it. We're the most ruthless (toward him!) as far as his comments, his writings, are concerned, I thought, if we don't have any more of his writings, because he *prudently* destroyed them, we go after his comments in order to destroy him, I thought. We exploit his unpublished papers in order to destroy even more the one who left them to us, to make the dead man even deader, and if he hasn't left us the appropriate instructions to destroy his papers, we invent them, simply invent declarations against him, etc., I thought. Heirs are cruel, the survivors don't have the slightest consideration, I thought. We're searching for testimony against him, for us, I thought. We plunder everything that can be used against him in order to improve our situation, I thought, that's the truth. Wertheimer had always been a candidate for suicide, but he overdrew his account, he should have killed himself years *before* his actual suicide, long before Glenn, I thought. This way his suicide is an embarrassment, above all mean-spirited, since he killed himself right in front of his sister's house in Zizers, I thought, above all in reaction to my bad conscience, which was still troubled by the fact that I hadn't answered Wertheimer's letters, had more or less ignominiously abandoned him, that I couldn't get away from Madrid had been a mean lie I used not to give myself up to my friend who, as I now see, had hoped to receive from me his last chance of survival, who before committing suicide had sent me four letters in Madrid that I didn't answer, I answered only the fifth, saying I absolutely couldn't budge, couldn't destroy my work merely for a trip to Austria, no matter for what reason. I had put *About Glenn Gould* first, that bungled essay which, as I now thought, I'll throw in the stove the minute I get back to Madrid because it doesn't have the slightest value. I ignominiously abandoned Wertheimer, I thought, in his greatest need I turned my back on him. But I vehemently repressed the thought of my own guilt in his suicide, I wouldn't have been able to help him, I told myself, I couldn't have saved him, he was of course already ripe for suicide. It must have been his school, I thought, which was a music school to boot! At first we thought we'd become famous and indeed in the easiest and fastest way possible, for which of course a music conservatory is the ideal springboard, that's how the three of us saw it, Glenn, Wertheimer and I. But only Glenn succeeded in doing what all three of us had planned, in the end Glenn even misused us for his own purposes, I thought, misused everybody in order to become Glenn Gould, although unconsciously, I thought. The two of us, Wertheimer and myself, had had to give up to make room for Glenn. At the time I didn't find this thought as absurd as it now seems to me, I thought. But Glenn was already a genius when he came to Europe and took Horowitz's course, we were already failures then, I thought. In reality I hadn't wanted to become a piano virtuoso, everything at the Mozarteum and everything connected with it had been only a pretext for me to save myself from my actual boredom with the world, from my very early satiety with life. And in reality Wertheimer behaved as I did, that's why nothing came of us, as they say, since we hadn't even been thinking of becoming somebody, in contrast to Glenn, who wanted to become Glenn Gould at all costs and who only needed to come to Europe to misuse Horowitz to be the genius he had longed and wished to be as he had wished for nothing else, a pianistic *world flabbergaster* so to speak. I took pleasure in this term *world flabbergaster*, while still standing in the restaurant and waiting for the innkeeper, who, to judge from the sound coming from behind the inn, was probably busy feeding the pigs behind the inn, as I thought. I myself had never felt *the need to be a world flabbergaster*, nor had Wertheimer, I thought. Wertheimer's head was more like mine than Glenn's, I thought, Glenn had an absolute virtuoso head on his shoulders, unlike Wertheimer and me, who had intellectual heads. But if I now had to define what a virtuoso head is, I couldn't define it any more than I could an intellectual head. Wertheimer hadn't befriended Glenn Gould, I had, I had approached and befriended Glenn, that's when Wertheimer came to us, and at bottom Wertheimer always remained an outsider among us. But all three of us were, as one can say, *friends for life*, I thought. Wertheimer seriously hurt his sister with the mere fact of his suicide, I thought, from now on that hole-in-the-wall called Zizers will count the brother's suicide against the wife of the chemical-plant owner, I thought, and the impudence of hanging oneself from a tree in front of one's sister's house will have even more damaging consequences for her. Wertheimer put no store in *funereal rites*, I thought, but he never would have received any in Chur, where he was buried. Significantly enough the funeral took place at five in the morning, besides the employees of a funeral

parlor in Chur the only ones in attendance were
Wertheimer's sister, her husband and myself.
Whether I would like to see Wertheimer one last
time, I was asked (strangely enough by Wertheimer's sister), but I refused immediately. The offer
disgusted me. As did the whole affair and those
involved in it. It would have been better not to go
to the funeral in Chur, I thought now. From the
telegram that Wertheimer's sister had sent me it
wasn't clear whether Wertheimer had committed
suicide, only the time of the funeral was mentioned. At first I had thought he died while visiting
his sister. Naturally I was surprised by this visit,
for I couldn't imagine such a thing. Wertheimer
would never have visited his sister in Zizers, I
thought. He's punished his sister with the maximum sentence, I thought, destroyed her brain for
life. The trip from Vienna to Chur took thirteen
hours, Austrian trains are a disaster, their dining
cars, assuming there is one, serve only the worst
food. A glass of mineral water set in front of me,
I planned to reread after twenty years Musil's *The
Confusions of Young Törless*, which however I
didn't manage, I no longer tolerate stories, I read
a page and can't read further. I no longer tolerate
descriptions. On the other hand I couldn't kill time
with Pascal either, I knew his *Pensées* by heart and
the pleasure afforded by Pascal's style was soon
over. So I contented myself with *observing* the
countryside. The towns all seem run-down when
seen from the train, the farmhouses have all been
ruined because their owners have replaced the old

windows with new, tasteless plastic windows.
Church spires no longer dominate the countryside,
imported plastic silos, oversized warehouse spires,
are everywhere. The ride from Vienna to Linz is
a trip through nothing but utter tastelessness.
From Linz to Salzburg things aren't much better.
And the Tyrolian mountains make me anxious.
I've always hated Vorarlberg, as I have Switzerland, where cretinism reigns supreme, as my father
always said, on this point I didn't disagree with
him. I knew Chur from my frequent visits there
with my parents, that is, when we were traveling
to St. Moritz and would spend the night in Chur,
always in the same hotel, which stank of pepper-
mint tea and where the hotel management knew
my father and gave him a twenty percent discount
because he had *remained faithful to the hotel for
over forty years*. It was a so-called good hotel, in
the center of town, I no longer remember the
name, perhaps it was the *Sunshine Inn*, if I'm not
mistaken, although it was located in the murkiest
spot in town. The taverns in Chur served the worst
wine and the most tasteless sausages. My father
always had dinner with us in the hotel, ordered a
so-called appetizer and called Chur *a pleasant stop-
over point*, which I never understood, for I had
always found Chur particularly distasteful. Even
more than the Salzburgers, the Churians struck
me as despicable in their Alpine cretinism. I always
felt as if I were being punished when I had to go
to St. Moritz with my parents, sometimes only
with my father, had to stop over in Chur, had to

stay in that dreary hotel with windows looking out on a narrow, dank street. In Chur I had never been able to sleep, I thought, I had always lain awake in complete despair. Chur is actually the gloomiest place I've ever seen, not even Salzburg is as gloomy and, in the final analysis, as sickening as Chur. And the Churians are just the same. A person can be ruined for life in Chur, even if he spends only one night there. But even today it isn't possible to go by train from Vienna to St. Moritz in a single day, I thought. I was spending the night outside Chur because, as mentioned, I had such a depressing memory of Chur from my childhood. I simply stayed on the train past Chur and got out between Chur and Zizers where I had seen a sign for a hotel. *Blauer Adler,* I read the next morning, the day of the funeral, as I left the hotel. Of course I hadn't slept. Glenn wasn't actually crucial for Wertheimer's suicide, I thought, it was his sister's moving out, her marriage with the Swiss. By the way, I had listened to Glenn's Goldberg Variations in my apartment in Vienna before leaving for Chur, over and over again from the beginning. Had got up again and again from my chair and paced up and down in my study, obsessed with the idea that Glenn was *actually* playing the Goldberg Variations in my apartment; while pacing back and forth I tried to discover the difference between his *interpretation* in *these* records and his *interpretation* twenty-eight years earlier for Horowitz and us, that is Wertheimer and myself, in the Mozarteum. I couldn't detect any difference.

Glenn had already played the Goldberg Variations twenty-eight years before exactly as he did in these records, which by the way he had sent me for my fiftieth birthday, he gave them to one of my New York friends as she was leaving for Vienna. I listened to him play the Goldberg Variations and remembered how he thought he'd immortalized himself with this interpretation, perhaps he's done it too, I thought, for I can't imagine that there will ever be a piano player who plays the Goldberg Variations like him, that is with as much genius as Glenn. I was listening to his Goldberg Variations for the sake of my work on Glenn and suddenly noticed the deplorable state of my apartment, which I hadn't entered for three years. Nor had anyone else entered my apartment in that time, I thought. I had been gone for three years, had withdrawn completely in the Calle del Prado, hadn't been able to even imagine returning to Vienna in these three years and hadn't thought about it either, never again to Vienna, that profoundly despised city, to Austria, that profoundly despised country. That was my salvation, to leave Vienna forever so to speak, take up residence in Madrid, which has become the ideal center of my existence, not in time but from the very first moment I arrived, I thought. In Vienna I would have been devoured bit by bit, as Wertheimer always said, suffocated by the Viennese and generally destroyed by the Austrians. Everything about me is such that it had to be suffocated in Vienna and destroyed in Austria, I thought, just as Wertheimer also thought that the Viennese had to suffocate him, that the Austrians had to destroy him. But Wertheimer wasn't one to leave for Madrid or Lisbon or Rome at the drop of a hat, unlike me he wasn't up to that. So he was always left only with the possibility of escaping to Traich, but in Traich everything was even worse for him. Alone so to speak with the human sciences in Traich, he had to lose out, had to perish. Together with his sister, yes, but alone with his human sciences in Traich, no, I thought. He finally so hated the city of Chur, which he didn't know at all, hated the very name of the city of Chur, the word Chur, that he had to go there to kill himself, I thought. The word Chur just like the word *Zizers* finally forced him to go to Switzerland and string himself up from a tree, naturally from a tree not far from his sister's house. *Preordained* was one of his expressions, the idea fits his suicide exactly, I thought, *his suicide was preordained*, I thought. All my tendencies are deadly ones, he once said to me, everything in me has a deadly tendency to it, it's in my genes, as Wertheimer said, I thought. He always read books that were obsessed with suicide, with disease and death, I thought while standing in the inn, books that described human misery, the hopeless, meaningless, senseless world in which everything is always devastating and deadly. That's why he especially loved Dostoevsky and all his disciples, Russian literature in general, because it actually is a deadly literature, but also the depressing French philosophers. He most loved to read and study

medical texts, and again and again his walks took
him to hospitals and sanatoria, to nursing homes
and morgues. He kept this habit to the very end.
Although he feared hospitals and sanatoria and
nursing homes and morgues, he always went into
these hospitals and sanatoria and nursing homes
and morgues. And if he didn't go to a hospital
because he couldn't, he would read articles or
books about sick people and diseases, and books
or articles about the terminally ill if he didn't have
the opportunity to go to a sanatorium for the terminally ill, or read articles and books about old
people if he couldn't visit a nursing home, and
articles and books about the dead if he hadn't had
the opportunity to visit a morgue. Naturally we
want to have a practical relationship with the
things that fascinate us, he once said, that is above
all a relationship with the sick and the terminally
ill and the old and the dead, because a theoretical
relationship isn't enough, but for long periods we
depend on a theoretical relationship, just as we
often depend on a theoretical relationship as far as
music is concerned, so Wertheimer, I thought. He
was fascinated with people in their unhappiness,
not with people themselves but with their unhappiness, and he found it wherever there were people, I thought, he was addicted to people because
he was addicted to unhappiness. Man is unhappiness, he said over and over, I thought, only an
idiot would claim otherwise. To be born is to be
unhappy, he said, and as long as we live we re-
produce this unhappiness, only death puts an end

to it. That doesn't mean that we are only unhappy, our unhappiness is the precondition for the fact that we can also be happy, only through the detour of unhappiness can we be happy, he said, I thought. My parents have never shown me anything but unhappiness, he said, that's the truth, I thought, and yet they were always happy, so he couldn't say that his parents had been unhappy people, just as he couldn't say they'd been happy, just as he couldn't say of himself he'd been a happy person or an unhappy one, because all people are simultaneously unhappy and happy, and sometimes unhappiness is greater in them than happiness and vice versa. But the fact remains that people are more unhappy than happy, he said, I thought. He was an *aphorism writer*, there are countless aphorisms of his, I thought, one can assume he destroyed them, *I write aphorisms*, he said over and over, I thought, that is a minor art of the intellectual asthma from which certain people, above all in France, have lived and still live, so-called half philosophers for nurses' night tables, I could also say calendar philosophers for everybody and anybody, whose sayings eventually find their way onto the walls of every dentist's waiting room; the so-called depressing ones are, like the so-called cheerful ones, equally disgusting. But I haven't been able to get rid of my habit of writing aphorisms, in the end I'm afraid I will have written millions of them, he said, I thought, and I'd be well advised to start destroying them since I don't plan to have the walls of every dentist's office and church papered with them one day, as they are now with Goethe, Lichtenberg and comrades, he said, I thought. Since I wasn't born to be a philosopher I turned myself into an aphorist, not entirely unconsciously I must say, turned myself into one of those disgusting tagalongs of philosophy who exist by the thousands, he said, I thought. To produce a huge effect with tiny ideas and deceive mankind, he said, I thought. In reality I'm nothing other than one of those aphorizing public menaces who, in their boundless unscrupulousness and impudence, tag along behind philosophers like horseflies behind a horse, he said, I thought. If we stop drinking we die of thirst, if we stop eating we starve to death, he said, such pearls of wisdom are what all these aphorisms amount to in the end, that is unless they're by Novalis, but even Novalis talked a lot of nonsense, so Wertheimer, I thought. In the desert we thirst for water, that's about what Pascal's maxim says, he said, I thought. If we look at things squarely the only thing left from the greatest philosophical enterprises is a pitiful aphoristic aftertaste, he said, no matter what the philosophy, no matter what the philosopher, everything falls to bits when we set to work with all our faculties and that means with all our mental instruments, he said, I thought. All this time I've been talking about the human sciences and don't even know what these human sciences are, don't have the slightest clue, he said, I thought, been talking about philosophy and don't have a clue about philosophy, been talking about existence and don't have a clue about it, he said. Our starting point is always that we don't know anything about anything and don't even have a clue about it, he said, I thought. Immediately after setting to work on something we choke on the huge amount of information that's available in all fields, that's the truth, he said, I thought. And although we know that, we continue to set to work on our so-called human-science problems, to attempt the impossible: *to create a human-science product, a product of the intellect. That's madness!* he said, I thought. Fundamentally we are capable of everything, equally fundamentally we fail at everything, he said, I thought. Our great philosophers, our greatest poets, shrivel down to a single successful sentence, he said, I thought, that's the truth, often we remember only a so-called philosophical hue, he said, I thought. We study a monumental work, for example Kant's work, and in time it shrivels down to Kant's little East Prussian head and to a thoroughly amorphous world of night and fog, which winds up in the same state of helplessness as all the others, he said, I thought. He wanted it to be a monumental world and only a single ridiculous detail is left, he said, I thought, that's how it always is. In the end the so-called great minds wind up in a state where we can only feel pity for their ridiculousnes, their pitifulness. Even Shakespeare shrivels down to something ridiculous for us in a clearheaded moment, he said, I thought. For a long time now the gods appear to us only in the heads on our beer steins, he said, I thought.

Only a stupid person is amazed, he said, I thought. The so-called intellectual consumes himself in what he considers pathbreaking work and in the end has only succeeded in making himself ridiculous, whether he's called Schopenhauer or Nietzsche, it doesn't matter, even if he was Kleist or Voltaire we still see a pitiful being who has misused his head and finally driven himself into nonsense. Who's been rolled over and passed over by history. We've locked up the great thinkers in our bookcases, from which they keep staring at us, sentenced to eternal ridicule, he said, I thought. Day and night I hear the chatter of the great thinkers we've locked up in our bookcases, these ridiculous intellectual giants as shrunken heads behind glass, he said, I thought. All these people have sinned against nature, he said, they've committed first-degree murders *of the intellect*, that's why they've been punished and stuck in our bookcases for eternity. For they're choking to death in our bookcases, that's the truth. Our libraries are so to speak prisons where we've locked up our intellectual giants, naturally Kant has been put in solitary confinement, like Nietzsche, like Schopenhauer, like Pascal, like Voltaire, like Montaigne, all the real giants have been put in solitary confinement, all the others in mass confinement, but everyone for ever and ever, my friend, for all time and unto eternity, that's the truth. And should one of these first-degree criminals of the intellect attempt to flee, break loose, he is immediately ridiculed and finished off, so to speak, that's the truth. Mankind knows how to protect itself against all these so-called intellectual giants, he said, I thought. The mind, wherever it makes its claims felt, is finished off and locked up and of course immediately branded as *mindless*, he said, I thought while looking up at the restaurant ceiling. But everything we say is nonsense, he said, I thought, no matter what we say it is nonsense and our entire life is a single piece of nonsense. I understood that early on, I'd barely started to think for myself and I already understood that, we speak only nonsense, everything we say is nonsense, but everything that is *said* to us is also nonsense, like everything that is said at all, in this world only nonsense has been said until now and, he said, only nonsense has actually and naturally been written, the writings we possess are only nonsense because they can only be nonsense, as history proves, he said, I thought. In the end *I fled into the notion of the aphorist*, he said, and when asked my profession I actually once responded, so Wertheimer said, that I was an *aphorist*. But people didn't understand what I meant, as usual, when I say something they don't understand it, for what I say doesn't mean that I said what I said, he said, I thought. I say something, he said, I thought, and I'm saying something completely different, thus I've spent my entire life in misunderstandings, in nothing but misunderstandings, he said, I thought. We are, to put it precisely, born into misunderstanding and never escape this condition of misunderstanding as long as we live, we can squirm and twist as much as we like, it doesn't help. But everyone can see this, he said, I thought, for everyone says something repeatedly and is misunderstood, this is the only point where everybody understands everybody else, he said, I thought. One misunderstanding casts us into the world of misunderstanding, which we must put up with as a world composed solely of misunderstandings and which we depart from with a single great misunderstanding, for death is the greatest misunderstanding of all, so Wertheimer, I thought. Wertheimer's parents were small people, Wertheimer himself was bigger than his parents, I thought. He was of impressive stature, as they say, I thought. In Hietzing alone the Wertheimers owned three princely villas and when Wertheimer once had to decide if he wanted to have one of his father's villas in Grinzing put in his name or not, Wertheimer let his father know that he didn't have the slightest interest in this villa, nor indeed any interest in the other villas owned by his father, who also had several factories in Lobau, not to mention the companies in the rest of Austria and abroad, I thought. The Wertheimers have always lived, as the saying goes, *in grand style,* but no one noticed it because they had never let anyone notice it, one couldn't see how wealthy they were, at least not at first glance. Basically the Wertheimer children hadn't had the slightest interest in their inheritance, and when their parents' will was opened neither Wertheimer nor his sister had had the slightest notion of the dimensions of the property that suddenly fell into their hands, the list of properties that a lawyer from Vienna's First District had drawn up hardly interested either of them, although they were surprised by the *actual* wealth that was suddenly theirs but that they considered a cumbersome burden. Except for the Kohlmarkt apartment and the hunting lodge in Traich they had everything sold and had the money deposited in banks throughout the world by a lawyer who belonged to the family, as Wertheimer put it, for once breaking his habit of never speaking about his financial situation. Three fourths of the parents' property went to Wertheimer, a fourth to his sister, she too had her inheritance deposited in various banking establishments in Austria, Germany and Switzerland, I thought. The Wertheimer children were financially secure, I thought, as I also am by the way, although my own financial situation could not be compared with that of Wertheimer and his sister. Wertheimer's great-grandparents had been dirt poor, I thought, farmers who twisted goose necks in the villages outside Lvov. But like me he came from a family of merchants, I thought. For one of his birthdays his father had the idea of giving him a castle in the Marchfeld that once belonged to the Harrachs, but his son wasn't even willing to take a look at the castle that he already owned, at which point his father, naturally enraged by his son's indifference, sold it, I thought. Basically the Wertheimer children led a modest life, unpretentious, unostentatious, more or less in the background, although everyone else in their

circle was always putting on airs. At the Mozarteum people didn't notice Wertheimer's wealth either. Nor did they notice Glenn's wealth by the
way, and Glenn was wealthy. Retrospectively it
was clear that the wealthy had found each other,
I thought, they had a sixth sense for their mutual
background. Glenn's genius was then so to speak
just a welcome extra, I thought. Friendships, I
thought, as experience shows, are finally only possible when they are based on mutual backgrounds,
I thought, all other conclusions are false. I was
suddenly astonished by the cold-bloodedness with
which I got off the train in Attnang-Puchheim to
go to Wankham and then Traich, to Wertheimer's
hunting lodge, without even thinking of visiting
my own house in Desselbrunn, which for five
years has been standing empty and which I assume,
since I pay the appropriate people, gets aired out
every four or five days; astonished by my cold-
blooded wish to spend the night here in Wankham
in the most disgusting inn I know, when not twelve
kilometers away I have my own house, but which
I won't visit under any circumstances, as I immediately thought, for I vowed to myself five years
ago not to go to Desselbrunn for at least ten years,
and until now I hadn't had any difficulty in keeping this vow, that is in controlling myself. Through
constant self-sacrifice I had thoroughly ruined life
in Desselbrunn for myself, one day it suddenly
became completely unbearable, I thought. The beginning of this self-sacrifice had been the rejection
of my Steinway, the triggering moment so to speak

for my subsequent inability to tolerate life in Desselbrunn. All at once I could no longer breathe the Desselbrunn air and the walls in Desselbrunn made me sick and the rooms threatened to choke me, one has to remember how cavernous the rooms are there, nine-by-six-meter or eight-by-eight-meter rooms, I thought. I hated those rooms and I hated what was in those rooms and when I left my house I hated the people outside my house, all at once I was being unjust to all those people, who only wanted *the best for me*, but precisely that drove me crazy after a while, their constant *willingness to be helpful*, which I suddenly found profoundly revolting. I barricaded myself in my study and stared out the window, without seeing anything but my own unhappiness. I ran outdoors and cursed at everybody. I ran into the woods and huddled beneath a tree, exhausted. To avoid actually going insane, I turned my back on Desselbrunn, *for at least ten years, for at least ten years, for at least ten years*, I repeated to myself without interruption as I left the house and went to Vienna to go to Portugal, where I had relatives in Sintra, in the most beautiful region of Portugal, where the eucalyptus trees grow thirty meters high and you can breathe the best air. In Sintra I'll find my way back to music, which in Desselbrunn I had driven out of myself thoroughly and so to speak for all time, I thought then, I thought, and I will regenerate myself by breathing the Atlantic air at mathematically calculated intervals. At that time I had also thought I could resume playing my Sintra uncle's Steinway where I'd left off in Desselbrunn, but that was a ridiculous thought, I thought, in Sintra I ran six kilometers down the Atlantic coast every day and for eight months didn't think about touching a piano, while my uncle and all the others in his house kept saying I should play something for them, in Sintra I never even touched a key, of course in Sintra during this admittedly wonderful inactivity in the fresh air and, as I have to say, in one of the most beautiful areas *of the world*, I came upon the idea of writing something about Glenn, *something*, I couldn't know what, *something about him and his art*. With this thought I walked up and down in Sintra and the surroundings and finally spent a whole year there without getting beyond this *something about Glenn*. To start to write is the hardest thing of all and for months and even years I ran around with this thought of writing something without being able to begin, something about Glenn who, as I thought then, had to be described, described of course by a competent witness of his existence, not just of his piano playing, by a competent witness of his thoroughly extraordinary intellect. One day I dared to begin this work, in the *Inglaterra* where I had wanted to stay only two days but where I spent six weeks in uninterrupted writing about Glenn. In the end however, when I moved to Madrid, I had only sketches for this work in my pocket and I destroyed these sketches because they suddenly became an obstacle to my work rather than a help, I had made too many sketches, this tendency has already ruined many of my works; we have to make sketches for a work, but if we make too many sketches we ruin everything, I thought, and so it was then in the *Inglaterra*, I sat in my room without interruption and made so many sketches that I thought I'd gone crazy and recognized that these Glenn-sketches were the cause of my insanity and I had the strength to destroy these Glenn-sketches. I simply put them in the wastepaper basket and watched the maid pick up the wastepaper basket and take it out of the room and make them disappear with the garbage. That was a pleasant sight, I thought, to see the maid pick up my Glenn-sketches, not only hundreds but thousands of them, and make them disappear. What a relief, I thought. I sat at my chair in front of the window for the entire afternoon, at dusk I was finally able to leave the *Inglaterra* and walk down the *Liberdade* in Lisbon and go to the Rua Garrett to my favorite bar. I had eight such false starts behind me, all of which ended by my destroying the sketches, before I finally realized in Madrid *how* I had to begin the work *About Glenn*, which I then finished in the Calle del Prado, I thought. But already I doubted whether this work was truly worth something and was thinking of destroying it upon my return, everything we write down, if we leave it for a while and start reading it from the beginning, naturally becomes unbearable and we won't rest until we've destroyed it again, I thought. Next week I'll be in Madrid again and the first thing I'll do is destroy my *Glenn Essay* in order to start a new one, I thought, an even more intense, even more authentic one, I thought. For we always think we are authentic and in truth are not, we think we're intense and in truth are not. But of course this insight has always resulted in none of my works ever being published, I thought, not a single one in the twenty-eight years I've been writing, just the work about Glenn has kept me busy for nine years, I thought. How good it is that none of these imperfect, incomplete works has ever appeared, I thought, had I published them, which would have posed no difficulty whatsoever, today I would be the unhappiest person imaginable, confronted daily with disastrous works crying out with errors, imprecision, carelessness, amateurishness. I *avoided* this punishment *by destroying them*, I thought, and suddenly I took great pleasure in the word *destroying*. Several times I said it to myself out loud. *Arrival in Madrid, immediately destroy my Glenn Essay*, I thought, I must get rid of it as quickly as possible to make room for a new one. Now I know *how* to set about this work, I never knew how, I always began too soon, I thought, like an amateur. All our lives we run away from amateurishness and it always catches up with us, I thought, we want nothing with greater passion than to escape our lifelong amateurishness and it always catches up with us. *Glenn and ruthlessness, Glenn and solitude, Glenn and Bach, Glenn and the Goldberg Variations*, I thought. *Glenn in his studio in the woods, his hatred of people, his hatred of music, his music-people hatred*, I thought. *Glenn and simplicity*, I thought while contemplating the restaurant. We have to know what we want right from the start, I thought, already as children we have to be clear in our minds what it is we want, want to have, have to have, I thought. The time I spent in Desselbrunn, and Wertheimer in Traich, I thought, was deadly. Our mutual visits and mutual criticism, I thought, which destroyed us. I only visited Wertheimer in Traich to destroy him, to disturb and destroy him, just as vice versa Wertheimer visited me for no other reason; to go to Traich merely signified a distraction from my horrible mental misery and the chance to disturb Wertheimer, our exchange of childhood memories, I thought, over a cup of tea, and always Glenn Gould at the center, not Glenn but Glenn Gould, who destroyed us both, I thought. Wertheimer came to Desselbrunn to disturb me, to ruin a work I'd started at the very moment he announced himself. He kept repeating, *if only we hadn't met Glenn*, but also, *if Glenn had died early, before he became a world celebrity*, I thought. We meet a person like Glenn and are destroyed, I thought, or rescued, in our case Glenn destroyed us, I thought. I would never have played on a Bösendorfer, said Glenn, I thought, I would never have gotten anywhere on a Bösendorfer. The Bösendorfer players against the Steinway players, I thought, the Steinway enthusiasts against the Bösendorfer enthusiasts. At first they brought a Bösendorfer to his room, he had it removed immediately, exchanged for a Steinway, I thought,

I wouldn't have dared to be so demanding, I thought, back then in Salzburg at the very start of our Horowitz course; even then Glenn was already completely self-assured, for him a Bösendorfer was simply out of the question, would have ruined his plan. And without protest they had exchanged the Bösendorfer for the Steinway, I thought, although Glenn wasn't yet Glenn Gould. I can still see the movers who carried out the Bösendorfer and carried in the Steinway, I thought. But Salzburg is no place for a piano player to develop, Glenn often said, the air is too damp, it ruins the instrument and at the same time it ruins the piano player, ruins a player's hands and head in the shortest time. But I wanted to study with Horowitz, Glenn said, that was the decisive thing. In Wertheimer's room the curtains were always drawn and the shutters closed, Glenn played with the curtains and shutters open, I always played with the windows open. Luckily there were no adjacent houses and as a result no one was up in arms against us, for that would have ruined our work. For the duration of our Horowitz course we had rented the house of a recently deceased Nazi sculptor, the *creations of the master*, as he was called in the area, still stood all over the house, in rooms that were five to six meters high. It was the height of these rooms that had convinced us to rent the house *on the spot*, the sculptures standing about didn't disturb us, they improved the acoustics, these marble eyesores along the walls that had been created by a *world-famous artist*, as we were told, who had worked for years in the service of Hitler. These giant marble protuberances, which the owners actually pushed against the walls for us, were acoustically ideal, I thought. At first we were shocked by the sight of the sculptures, by this cretinous marble and granite monumentality, Wertheimer especially cowered before them, but Glenn immediately claimed the rooms to be *ideal*, and because of the monuments *even more ideal for our purpose*. The sculptures were so heavy that our attempt to move even the smallest of them failed, our combined forces weren't enough, and we were no weaklings, piano virtuosos are strong people with amazing endurance, quite contrary to common opinion. Glenn, whom even today people assume to have had the weakest constitution, was an athletic type. Hunched over his Steinway, he looked like a cripple, that's how the entire musical world knows him, but this entire musical world is prey to a total misconception, I thought. Glenn is portrayed everywhere as a cripple and a weakling, as the *transcendent artist* his fans can accept only with his infirmity and the hypersensitivity that goes along with this infirmity, but actually he was an athletic type, much stronger than Wertheimer and me put together, we realized that at once when he went out to chop down an ash tree with his own hands, an ash tree in front of his window, which, as he put it, obstructed his playing. He cut down the ash, which had a diameter of at least a half meter, all by himself, didn't even let us get near the ash, chopped the ash into smaller pieces at once and stacked them against the house, the typical American, I had thought then, I thought. Glenn had barely cut down the ash that supposedly obstructed his playing when he had the idea of simply drawing the curtains in his room, closing the shutters. I could have spared myself the work of cutting down the ash, he said, I thought. We often cut down such an ash, a whole forest of such mental ashes, he said, and we could have spared ourselves the work with a simple sleight of hand, he said, I thought. The ash in front of his window disturbed him the minute he sat down at his Steinway in Leopoldskron. Without even asking the owners he went to the toolshed, grabbed an ax and a saw and chopped down the ash. If I have to spend time asking, he said, I just lose time and energy, I'm going to chop down the ash at once, he said, and chopped it down, I thought. The ash was barely on the ground when he realized that he had only needed to draw the curtains, close the shutters. He cut the felled ash into pieces without our help, I thought, created the perfect order he needed where the ash had once stood. If something is in our way we have to get rid of it, Glenn said, even if it's only an ash. And we don't even have the right to ask first if we are allowed to chop down the ash, we weaken ourselves that way. If we ask first we're already so weakened that it's bad for us, may even destroy us, he said, I thought. Not one of his fans, his worshipers, as I immediately thought again, would ever think that Glenn Gould, who is known and famous in the whole world so to speak as the absolute weakling of artists, could cut down a strong, healthy, half-meter-thick ash by himself and in the shortest time and stack the pieces of this ash against the house, in dreadful atmospheric conditions to boot, I thought. His worshipers worship a phantom, I thought, they worship a Glenn Gould that never existed. But *my* Glenn Gould is incomparably greater, more deserving of worship, I thought, than theirs. When we learned that we had moved into the house of a famous Nazi sculptor Glenn burst out laughing. Wertheimer joined in this resounding laughter, I thought, the two of them laughed to the point of total exhaustion and in the end they went down to the cellar to get a bottle of champagne. Glenn popped the cork right in the face of a six-meter-high Carrara angel and squirted the champagne at the faces of the other monsters standing about, leaving only a little bit which we drank from the bottle. Finally Glenn hurled the bottle at the emperor head in the corner with such fury that we had to duck for cover. Not one of these Glenn worshipers is capable of imagining Glenn Gould laughing the way he always laughed, I thought. Our Glenn Gould was capable of unbridled laughter like no other, I thought, and for that reason must be taken most seriously. Whoever can't laugh doesn't deserve to be taken seriously, I thought, and whoever can't laugh like Glenn doesn't deserve to be taken as seriously as Glenn. At around three in the morning he draped himself over the emperor's feet, completely exhausted, he with his Goldberg Variations, I thought. Again and again this image: Glenn pressed against the emperor's calf, staring at the floor. One couldn't speak to him. In the morning he was *born anew*, in his words. Every day I put on a new head, so he said, whereas the world thinks it's still the old one, so he said. Every other day Wertheimer ran to the Untersberg at five in the morning, luckily he had discovered an asphalt road that went to the foot of the Untersberg, then he ran back, I myself simply walked once around the house before break-fast, although in all weather and completely undressed before washing. Glenn only left the house to go to Horowitz and come back. Basically I hate nature, he said again and again. I myself appropriated this sentence and still repeat it to my-self today, will always repeat it, as I believe, I thought. *Nature is against me*, said Glenn, adopt-ing my own philosophical perspective, for I also always say this sentence, I thought. Our existence consists in always being against nature and setting to work against nature, said Glenn, setting to work against nature until we give up, for nature is stronger than we are, we who in arrogance have turned ourselves into *art products*. We aren't peo-ple after all, *we are art products, the piano player is an art product, a disgusting one*, he said in con-clusion. We are the ones who continually want to escape from nature, but we can't do it, naturally, he said, I thought, we get stuck halfway. Basically we want to be the piano, he said, not human beings

but the piano, all our lives we want to be the piano
and not a human being, flee from the human beings
we are in order to completely become the piano,
an effort which must fail, although we don't want
to believe it, he said. The ideal piano player (he
never said *pianist*!) is the one who wants to be the
piano, and I say to myself every day when I wake
up, I want to be the Steinway, not the person
playing the Steinway, I want to be the Steinway
itself. Sometimes we get close to this ideal, he said,
very close, at which point we think we've already
gone crazy, think we're on the highroad to madness, which we fear like nothing else. All his life
Glenn had wanted to be the Steinway itself, he
hated the notion of being *between* Bach and his
Steinway as a mere musical middleman and of one
day being ground to bits between Bach on one side
and his Steinway on the other, he said, I thought.
All my life I have dreaded being ground to bits
between Bach and Steinway and it requires the
greatest effort on my part to escape this dread, he
said. My ideal would be, *I would be the Steinway,
I wouldn't need Glenn Gould,* he said, I could,
by being the Steinway, make Glenn Gould totally
superfluous. But not a single piano player has ever
managed to make himself superfluous by *being*
Steinway, as Glenn said. To wake up one day *and
be Steinway and Glenn in one,* he said, I thought,
Glenn Steinway, Steinway Glenn, all for Bach. It's
possible that Wertheimer hated Glenn, it's possible
he hated me as well, I thought; this thought is
based on thousands, if not tens of thousands, of

observations concerning Wertheimer, as well as Glenn, as well as me. And I myself wasn't free of Glenn hatred, I thought, I hated Glenn every moment, loved him at the same time with the utmost consistency. For there's nothing more terrible than to see a person so magnificent that his magnificence destroys us and we must observe this process and put up with it and finally and ultimately also accept it, whereas we actually don't believe such a process is happening, far from it, until it becomes an irrefutable fact, I thought, when it's too late. Wertheimer and I had been necessary for Glenn's development, like everything else in his life, Glenn misused us, I thought in the inn. The arrogance with which Glenn set about everything, Wertheimer's fearful hesitation on the other hand, my reservations about everything and anything, I thought. Suddenly Glenn was *Glenn Gould*, everybody overlooked the moment of the Glenn Gould transformation, as I have to call it, even Wertheimer and I. For months Glenn had drawn us into the same diet, I thought, into his Horowitz fixation, for it actually was possible that I (not to mention Wertheimer) wouldn't have lasted through those two and a half Salzburg months with Horowitz on my own, that I would have given up without Glenn. Even Horowitz wouldn't have been Horowitz if Glenn had been missing, the one made the other possible and vice versa. It was a Horowitz course for Glenn, I thought, standing in the inn, nothing else. Glenn had made Horowitz into a genial teacher, not Horowitz Glenn into a genius, I thought. In those months in Salzburg Glenn made Horowitz into the ideal teacher for his genius and through his genius, I thought. We get inside music completely or not at all, Glenn often said, to Horowitz as well. But he alone knew what that meant, I thought. A Glenn has to come upon a Horowitz, I thought, and precisely at the single right moment. If this moment isn't the right one, what Glenn and Horowitz accomplished won't be accomplished. The teacher who isn't a genius is made into a teacher of genius by the student of genius at this precise moment for a very precise time period, I thought. But the real victim of this Horowitz course wasn't me, it was Wertheimer, who certainly would have become an exceptional, perhaps world-famous piano virtuoso without Glenn, I thought. Who made the mistake of going to Salzburg that year to study with Horowitz and be destroyed by Glenn, not by Horowitz. Of course Wertheimer had *wanted* to become a piano virtuoso, I didn't want it at all, I thought, my virtuosity at the piano had only been a way out for me, a procrastination maneuver for something that I've never been able to put my finger on, not even today; Wertheimer wanted it, I didn't want it, I thought, Glenn has him on his conscience, I thought. Glenn had played only a few bars and Wertheimer was already thinking about giving up, I remember it precisely, Wertheimer had entered the first-floor room in the Mozarteum assigned to Horowitz and had heard and seen Glenn, had stood still at the door, incapable of sitting down, had to be invited by Horowitz to sit down, couldn't sit down as long as Glenn was playing, only when Glenn stopped playing did Wertheimer sit down, he closed his eyes, I can still see it in every detail, I thought, couldn't utter a word. To put it sentimentally, that was the end, the end of the Wertheimerian virtuoso career. For a decade we study the instrument we have chosen for ourselves and then, after this arduous, more or less depressing decade, we hear a genius play a few bars and are washed up, I thought. Werthei-mer wouldn't admit it, not for years. But those few bars of Glenn's playing meant his end, I thought. Not for me, since even before meeting Glenn I had thought of giving up, pondered the senselessness of my efforts, wherever I went I had always been the best, being accustomed to this fact didn't prevent me from thinking of giving up, of breaking off something senseless, against all those who affirmed that I belonged to the best, but to belong to the best wasn't enough for me, I wanted *to be the best or not at all,* and so I gave it up, gave my Steinway to the schoolteacher's child in Altmünster, I thought. Wertheimer had put all his eggs in his piano virtuoso career, as I have to call it, I hadn't put any eggs in such a piano virtuoso career, that was the difference. For that reason *he* was *fatally* wounded by Glenn's Goldberg bars, *not I*. To be the best or not at all has always been my motto, in every respect. And so I finally wound up in the Calle del Prado in total anonym-ity, occupied with a writer's inanities. Wertheimer's goal was to be the piano virtuoso who proves his mastery to the musical world year in, year out, until he keels over, until, if I know Wertheimer, he turns into a doddering octogenarian. Glenn wrenched this goal away from him, I thought, when Glenn sat down and played the first bars of the Goldberg Variations. Wertheimer had *had* to hear him, I thought, he had *had* to be destroyed by Glenn. If I hadn't gone to Salzburg back then and hadn't wanted to study with Horowitz at all costs, I would have continued playing and I would have accomplished what I wanted, Wertheimer often said. But Wertheimer had to go to Salzburg and enroll in Horowitz's course, as they say. We are already destroyed and still we don't give up, I thought, Wertheimer is a good example of this fact, for years after having been destroyed by Glenn he didn't give up, I thought. And it wasn't even he who had the idea of parting with his Bösendorfer, I thought, first I had to give away my Steinway so that he could auction off his Bösendorfer, he would never have given away his Bösendorfer, he had to auction it off at the Dorotheum, that is just like him, I thought. I gave my Steinway away, he auctioned off his Bösendorfer, I thought, and that says everything. Everything about Wertheimer didn't come from Wertheimer himself, I said to myself now, everything about Wertheimer was always taken from somebody else, copied, he took everything from me, he copied me in everything, and so he even took my failure from me and copied it, I thought.

Only his suicide was his own decision and came completely from him, I thought, and so he may have experienced, as they say, a sense of triumph in the end. And perhaps thus, by committing suicide on his own so to speak, he had outstripped me in everything, I thought. Weak characters never turn into anything more than weak artists, I said to myself, Wertheimer confirms that theory absolutely, I thought. Wertheimer's nature was completely opposed to Glenn's nature, I thought, he had a so-called *artistic attitude*, Glenn Gould didn't need one. Whereas Wertheimer continually asked questions, Glenn didn't ask any questions at all, I never heard him ask a question, I thought. Wertheimer was always afraid of overtaxing his strength, it didn't even occur to Glenn that he could overtax his strength, Wertheimer was constantly apologizing for something that didn't even need an apology, whereas Glenn wasn't even familiar with the concept of apology, Glenn never apologized, although by conventional standards he constantly needed to apologize. Wertheimer always had to know what people thought of him, Glenn couldn't have cared less, as I also couldn't care less, Glenn and I were always indifferent to the opinions of our so-called peers. Wertheimer talked even when he had nothing to say, simply because being silent had become dangerous for him, Glenn was silent for the longest periods, as was I, I who like Glenn could be silent for days at a time, if not for weeks, like Glenn. The simple fear of not being taken seriously made our loser prattle on, I thought. And it probably was also due to his being left completely to his own devices in Vienna as well as in Traich, of walking through Vienna and, as he always said, not talking to his sister about anything, since *he never even once had a conversation* with his sister. He had shameless administrators, as he called them, who took care of his properties, and dealt with them only by correspondence. Thus Wertheimer was also perfectly capable of being silent and perhaps could even be silent longer than Glenn and myself, but in our midst he had to talk, I thought. The person who resided at one of the best addresses in the center of town loved nothing better than to hang out in Floridsdorf, in a blue-collar neighborhood that has become famous for its locomotive factory, in Kagran, in Kaisermühlen where the poorest of the poor are housed, in the so-called Alsergrund, or in Ottakring, such perversity, I thought. Out the back door in grubby clothes, in proletarian disguise, so as not to be detected on his information hunts, I thought. Standing for hours on the Floridsdorf bridge, he would observe the passersby, would stare into the brown water of the Danube, long since destroyed by chemicals, stare at Russian and Yugoslavian freighters heading toward the Black Sea. There he often wondered, he said, whether it hadn't been his greatest misfortune to have been born into a wealthy family, I thought, for he always said he felt more at ease in Floridsdorf and in Kagran than in the First District, more at ease with the people in Floridsdorf and Kagran than with the people in the First District, whom he basically had always hated. He frequented bars in the Pragerstrasse and the Brünnerstrasse where he ordered beer and cheap sausage, sat for hours listening to people, observing them, until he was out of air as it were, until he had to get out, go home, naturally by foot, I thought. But over and over he also said it would be a mistake to think he'd be happier living in Floridsdorf, in Kagran, in the Alsergrund, I thought, it would be a mistake to assume these people had a better character than the people in the First District. Upon closer inspection, so he said, the so-called disadvantaged, the so-called poor and so-called retarded, were equally without character, had an equally repulsive nature, and should be rejected just as categorically as those in the social group we belong to and whom we judge to be repulsive only for this reason. The lower classes are just as much a public menace as the upper classes, he said, they commit the same hideous acts, should be rejected just as categorically as the others, they're different but they're equally hideous, he said, I thought. The so-called intellectual hates his so-called intellectualism and thinks he can find an answer with the so-called poor and disadvantaged, who used to be called the *downtrodden and despised*, he said, but instead of an answer he finds the same hideousness, he said, I thought. After visiting Floridsdorf and Kagran twenty or thirty times, so Wertheimer often said, I recognized my mistake and went to the *Bristol* instead and watched people of my own kind.

Again and again we try to escape ourselves, but we fail in our efforts, constantly run our heads into the wall because we don't want to recognize that we can't escape ourselves, except in death. Now he's escaped himself, I thought, and in a more or less unappetizing manner. To stop at fifty, fifty-one at the latest, he once said. In the end he took himself *seriously*, I thought. We observe a fellow student walking in the corridor, I thought, and address him and have started a so-called life-long friendship. Naturally we don't know right away that it is a so-called lifelong friendship because at first we experience it only as an interested friendship, one that we have to have at that moment to get ahead, but then again it's not just any person we've addressed but the only possible one at that moment, I thought, for I had hundreds of opportunities to address other students, who all studied at the Mozarteum and many of whom had taken Horowitz's course back then, but I addressed Wertheimer and no one else, reminding him that we had once met and spoken with each other in Vienna, I thought, which he remembered. Wertheimer studied primarily in Vienna, not like me at the Mozarteum, but at the Vienna Academy, which the Mozarteum has always considered the better music conservatory, just as the Vienna Academy has always considered the Mozarteum the more useful school, I thought. Students always judge their own school to be something less than it is and cast an envious glance at their rival school, above all music students are known for always giving much higher marks to their rival schools than to their own, and the Viennese music students always thought and believed the Mozarteum to be better, just as the Mozarteum students thought the Vienna Academy was better. Basically the Vienna Academy and the Mozarteum had and have always had equally good or equally bad teachers, I thought, it has always been up to the students to exploit these teachers with extreme ruthlessness for their own purposes. It doesn't even depend on the quality of our teachers, I thought, it's up to us, for even bad teachers have always produced geniuses in the end, just as good teachers have destroyed geniuses, I thought. Horowitz had a sterling reputation, we had answered the call of this sterling reputation, I thought. But we had no idea of Glenn Gould, what he meant for us. Glenn Gould was a student like everyone else, initially endowed with remarkable promise, finally with the greatest talent that has ever existed in this century, I thought. For me taking Horowitz's course wasn't the catastrophe it was for Wertheimer, Wertheimer was too weak for Glenn. Seen that way, Wertheimer, by enrolling in Horowitz's course, walked into a *trap for life*, I thought. The trap snapped shut the first time he heard Glenn play, I thought. Wertheimer never got out of this trap for life. Wertheimer should have stayed in Vienna and continued studying at the Vienna Academy, the word Horowitz destroyed him, I thought, indirectly the *concept Horowitz*, even if Glenn actually destroyed him. When we were in

America I told Glenn that he had destroyed Wertheimer, but Glenn had no idea what I meant. Never again did I bother him with this thought. Wertheimer had gone to America only against his will, during the trip he continually let me know that he basically detested artists who, in Wertheimer's own words, had taken their art as far as Glenn had, who destroyed their personalities to be geniuses, as Wertheimer expressed himself then. In the end people like Glenn had turned themselves into *art machines*, had nothing in common with human beings anymore, only seldom reminded you of human beings, I thought. But Wertheimer continually envied Glenn this art, he wasn't capable of marveling at it without envy, even if not admiring it, for which I also lacked and still lack all capacity, I've never admired anything but have marveled at many things during my life and, I can say, have marveled most in my life, which perhaps deserves the name of an artist's life, at Glenn, with true enthusiasm I marveled at his development, I marveled at him again and again, absorbed, as they say, his interpretations, I thought. I was always capable of letting my sense of marvel roam free, not letting myself be limited, hemmed in, by anybody or anything in my sense of marvel, I thought. Wertheimer never had this ability, in absolutely no respect, I thought. Unlike Wertheimer, who quite probably would have liked to be Glenn Gould, I never wanted to be Glenn Gould, I always only wanted to be myself, but Wertheimer belongs to the kind of person who constantly and all his life and to his constant despair wants to be someone else, someone, as he always believes, more favored in life, I thought. Wertheimer would have liked to be Glenn Gould, would have liked to be Horowitz, probably also would have liked to be Gustav Mahler or Alban Berg. Wertheimer wasn't capable of seeing *himself as a unique and autonomous being*, as people can and must if they don't want to despair; no matter what kind of person, one is always a unique and autonomous being, I say to myself over and over, and am rescued. Wertheimer was never able to seize hold of this rescue anchor, that is to consider himself a unique and autonomous being, he lacked all capacity for that. Every person is a unique and autonomous person and actually, considered independently, the greatest artwork of all time, I've always thought that and should have thought that, I thought. Wertheimer didn't have that possibility, and so he always only wanted to be Glenn Gould or, yes, Gustav Mahler or Mozart and comrades, I thought. That plunged him into unhappiness at a very early stage, again and again. We don't have to be a genius to be a unique and autonomous being and to be able to recognize that, I thought. Wertheimer was an unrelieved *emulator*, he emulated anybody he thought was better off than he was, although he didn't have the capacity for that, as I now see, I thought, he'd absolutely wanted to be an artist and thus walked into the mouth of disaster. Hence also his restlessness, his constant urgent walking, running, his inability to stand still, I thought. And he took his unhappiness out on his sister, whom he tormented for decades, I thought, locked away in his head, as it seemed to me, never again to let her out. At the so-called *recital evenings*, which students in the concert business are used to and which all take place in the so-called *Wiener Saal*, we once performed together, *playing Brahms for four hands*, as they say. Throughout the concert Wertheimer had wanted to assert himself and thus thoroughly wrecked the concert. Wrecked it absolutely on purpose, as I see today. After the concert he said *excuse me* and these two words were just like him. He was incapable of playing with someone else, he had wanted, as they say, to *shine*, and because naturally he couldn't manage it, he wrecked the concert, I thought. All his life Wertheimer always wanted to assert himself, something he's never managed to do, in no way, under no circumstances. As a result he had to kill himself, I thought. Glenn wouldn't have had to kill himself, I thought, for Glenn had never had to assert himself, he simply asserted himself always and everywhere and under all circumstances. Wertheimer always wanted more without being up to it, I thought, Glenn was up to everything. I'm not putting myself in question here, but for my part I can say that I was always capable of everything possible, but on the whole purposely avoided using this capacity, always out of indolence, arrogance, laziness, boredom, I thought. But Wertheimer never was up to anything he attempted, nothing and double nothing, as they say. Except that he was up to being an unhappy person. In this respect it's not surprising that Wertheimer killed himself and Glenn didn't and I didn't, although Wertheimer predicted *my* suicide over and over, like so many others who always let me know that *they* knew *I* would kill myself. Wertheimer actually played better than all the other students at the Mozarteum, that has to be said, but after hearing Glenn that wasn't enough for him. The level Wertheimer played at can be reached by anyone who sets himself the goal of becoming famous, achieving mastery over his instrument, if he spends the necessary decades of work at his piano, I thought, but when he comes across a Glenn Gould and has heard *such* a Glenn Gould play, he's a broken man if he's like Wertheimer, I thought. Wertheimer's funeral didn't even last an hour. At first I had wanted to put on a so-called dark suit for his funeral, but then I decided to go to the funeral in my traveling clothes, it had suddenly struck me as ridiculous to adapt myself to a sartorial mourning convention I've always hated, as I have all sartorial conventions, so I went to the funeral in the clothes I had on when I started my trip to Chur, in my usual suit. At first I had thought I would walk to the Chur cemetery, but then I got into a taxi and had myself driven to the main gate. I had carefully pocketed the telegram from Wertheimer's sister, whose name is now Duttweiler, for it stated the exact time of the funeral. I'd thought that it was an accident, that

Wertheimer had perhaps been run over by a car in Chur, since I wasn't aware of Wertheimer having any acute or life-threatening illness I had considered every possible kind of accident, above all however traffic accidents, which are so common today, but it didn't occur to me that he could have committed suicide. Although this thought, as I now see, I thought, would have been the most logical one. That the Duttweiler woman sent the telegram to my address in Vienna and not to Madrid surprised me, for how could Wertheimer's sister have known that I was in Vienna and not in Madrid, I thought. It still isn't clear to me how she knew she could reach me in Vienna and not in Madrid, I thought. Perhaps she did have some contact with her brother before his suicide, I thought. Of course I also would have come from Madrid to Chur, I thought, even if that would have been more difficult. Or perhaps wouldn't have been, since Chur is a stone's throw from Zurich. I again showed several people my apartment in Vienna, which I've wanted to sell for years without ever finding the appropriate buyer, the ones who showed up this time were also out of the question. Either they don't want to pay the price I'm asking or they withdraw for other reasons. I had intended to sell my apartment in Vienna *as it stands*, that is everything in it, but for that all prospective buyers had to look me in the face and not one of them was able to look me in the face, as they say. I also wondered whether it wasn't senseless to part with my Vienna apartment just *now, in these difficult times*, to give it up in a time of total uncertainty. No one is selling now if they're not absolutely forced to, I thought, and I wasn't forced to sell my apartment. I still have Desselbrunn, I had always thought, I don't need the Vienna apartment, for I live in Madrid and I'm not planning to return to Vienna, ever, I had always thought, but then I saw the horrible faces of all those buyers and lost all idea of selling my Vienna apartment. And in the final analysis, I thought, Desselbrunn won't be enough in time, it's better to have one foot in Vienna and one in Desselbrunn, than to have just Desselbrunn, and I thought that in fact I wouldn't return to Desselbrunn, but I won't sell Desselbrunn either. I won't sell the Vienna apartment and I won't sell Desselbrunn, I'll give up the Vienna apartment, which of course I've already given up, just as I'll give up and have already given up Desselbrunn, but I won't sell Vienna or Desselbrunn, I thought, I don't need to. If I'm honest I actually have enough of a cushion not to have to sell Desselbrunn or Vienna, to sell nothing at all. I'd be an idiot to sell, I thought. And so I have Vienna and I have Desselbrunn, even if I don't use Vienna or Desselbrunn, I thought, but in the background I have Vienna and Desselbrunn and as a result my independence is a much greater independence than if I didn't have Vienna or Desselbrunn, or didn't have Vienna *and* Desselbrunn, I thought. The funerals that aren't supposed to be noticed are scheduled for five o'clock in the morning, I thought, and Frau Duttweiler as well as the cemetery officials in Chur had wanted to avoid any commotion with Wertheimer's funeral. Wertheimer's sister said several times that her brother's funeral was *merely provisional*, she intended one day *to transport* her brother to Vienna, to have his remains put in the Wertheimer family grave in the cemetery in Döbling. At the moment, however, transporting her brother was out of the question, she didn't say why, I thought. The Wertheimer crypt is one of the biggest in the Döbling cemetery, I thought. Perhaps *next fall* Wertheimer's sister, Frau Duttweiler, had said, I thought. Herr Duttweiler had worn tails, I thought, and led Wertheimer's sister to the grave, which had been dug completely at the other end of the Chur cemetery, that is at the edge of the garbage heap. Since no one said anything and the pallbearers lowered the coffin with Wertheimer into the grave with unbelievably quick and deft movements, the funeral didn't last more than twenty minutes. A man dressed in black who apparently worked for the funeral home, was undoubtedly also the owner of the funeral establishment, I thought, had wanted to say something, but Herr Duttweiler had cut his speech off even before he had begun his speech. I hadn't been able to buy flowers for the funeral, in my entire life I've never done that, the fact that the Duttweilers also hadn't brought any flowers was all the more depressing, probably, I thought, because Wertheimer's sister was of the opinion that flowers weren't fitting for her brother's funeral, and this opinion was correct, I thought, even if this fully flowerless funeral had a chilling effect on all present. Herr Duttweiler gave each pall-bearer two bills while they were still standing beside the open grave, which seemed a crude gesture but nonetheless fit the whole funeral procedure. Wertheimer's sister looked down in the grave, her husband didn't, I didn't either. I walked out of the cemetery behind Herr and Frau Duttweiler. Before the gate they both turned to me and extended an invitation to have lunch with them, which however I didn't accept. That certainly wasn't correct, I thought now in the inn. I probably could have learned something important and useful from both of them and particularly from Wertheimer's sister, I thought, but I took my leave and suddenly stood there alone. Chur no longer interested me and I went to the station and left for Vienna with the next train. It is completely natural that we should think about the deceased intensively after a funeral, especially if he was a close friend, even more especially if he was an intimate friend with whom we have been linked for decades, and a so-called school friend is always an extraordinary companion in our lives and existences because he is so to speak a *prime* witness to our situation in life, I thought, and throughout the trip through Buchs and across the Liechtenstein border my thoughts circled obsessively around Wertheimer. That he was actually born into a giant fortune, all his life hadn't had any use for this giant fortune, had always been unhappy with this giant fortune, I thought. That his parents had been unable, as they say, to open his eyes, that they were the ones who depressed the child, I thought. *I had a depressing childhood*, Wertheimer always said, *I had a depressing adolescence*, he said, *I had a depressing period in college, I had a father who depressed me, a mother who depressed me, depressing teachers, an environment that constantly depressed me*. That they (his parents and teachers) always wounded his feelings and equally neglected his mind, I thought. That he never had a home, I thought, still standing in the restaurant, because his parents didn't give him a home, because they weren't able to give him a home. That he had spoken of his family like no other because his kin hadn't been a family. That finally he hadn't hated anything more than his parents, whom he always characterized as his undoers and destroyers. That after the death of his parents, who had driven off a cliff in the area near Bressanone, he ultimately had no one but his sister because he had offended everybody else including me and had completely taken possession of his sister, I thought, in unscrupulous fashion. That he always asked for everything, never gave anything, I thought. That he went to the Floridsdorf bridge again and again to throw himself off without actually ever throwing himself off, that he studied music to become a piano virtuoso without becoming a piano virtuoso, that finally, as he himself always said, he fled into the human sciences without knowing what these human sciences were, I thought. That on the one hand he overestimated, on the other hand underestimated his possibilities, I thought. That he kept asking me for more than he gave me, I thought. That his demands on me, as on others, were always too high and that these demands of his could never be met and as a result he had to become unhappy, I thought. Wertheimer was born an unhappy person, he knew that, but like all unhappy people he didn't want to admit that he *had* to be unhappy, as he believed but others didn't, that depressed him, kept him locked up in his despair. *Glenn is a happy person, I'm an unhappy one,* he often said, to which I responded that one couldn't say Glenn was a happy person whereas he, Wertheimer, actually was an unhappy person. It's always correct to say that this or that person is an unhappy person, I said to Wertheimer, I thought, whereas it's never correct to say that this or that person is a happy one. But from Wertheimer's perspective Glenn Gould was always a happy person, as I was, as I know because he told me so often enough, I thought, reproached me for being happy or at least happier than he was, for most of the time he judged himself the unhappiest person on earth. That Wertheimer also did everything to be unhappy, to be that unhappy person he was always talking about, I thought, for without a doubt his parents had tried to make their son happy, again and again, but Wertheimer had always rejected them, as he also always rejected his sister when she tried to make him happy. Like anybody else, Wertheimer couldn't be an unhappy person every second, one who, as he thought, is completely possessed by his unhappiness. I remember that he was happy during our Horowitz course, took walks with me (and with Glenn) that made him happy, that he also managed to transform his solitude in Leopoldskron into a happy condition, as my observations show, I thought, but actually that was all over when he first heard Glenn play the Goldberg Variations, which at that time Wertheimer, as I know, never dared to play. I myself had attempted to play the Goldberg Variations at an early age and long before Glenn Gould, I was never afraid of them, unlike Wertheimer who always put off the Goldberg Variations for a rainy day so to speak, I thought, I never experienced this cowardice toward such a monumental work as the Goldberg Variations, never suffered from such cowardice, never racked my brains over such impudence, indeed never even worried about it, so that quite simply I began to practice them, and indeed years before the Horowitz course *dared* to play them, naturally by heart and not worse than many of our famous concert artists, but naturally not as well as I would have liked. Wertheimer was always an anxious type, for this serious reason fully unsuited for a virtuoso career, especially at the piano, for which one needs above all a radically fearless nature toward everything and anything, I thought. The virtuoso, especially the world virtuoso, must not fear anything, I thought, no matter what kind of virtuoso he is. Wertheimer's fear was always plain to see, he never was able to disguise it even lightly. One day his career plan has to fall apart, I thought, as indeed it did fall apart, and not even this falling apart of his plan to be an artist was his own, it was precipitated by my decision to part definitively with my Steinway and with my career as a virtuoso, I thought. That he took everything or almost everything from me, I thought, even everything that suited me but not him, much that was useful for me but had to hamper him, I thought. The emulator emulated me in everything, even when it quite apparently went against his own interests, I thought. I always only hampered Wertheimer, I thought, and as long as I live I won't be able to clear my head of this self-reproach, I thought. Wertheimer wasn't independent, I thought. In many respects more refined than me but, and this was his biggest mistake, ultimately endowed only *with false feelings*, actually a *loser*, I thought. Because he didn't have the courage to take from Glenn what was important for him, he took everything from me, which however didn't help him since he took nothing useful from me, only useless things, although I repeatedly reminded him of this fact, I thought. If he'd become a businessman and thus an able administrator of his parents' empire, I thought, he would have been happy, happy in his sense of the word, but he lacked the courage for such a decision, was incapable of performing *the small about-face* that I had often spoken of in his presence but that he never attempted. He wanted to be an artist, *an artist of life* wasn't enough for him, although precisely this concept provides everything we need to be happy if we think about it, I thought. Ultimately he was enamored of failure, if not even a little smitten, I thought, had clung to this failure of his until the end. I could actually say he was unhappy in his unhappiness but he would have been even more unhappy had he lost his unhappiness overnight, had it been taken away from him from one moment to the next, which is again proof that basically he wasn't unhappy at all but happy, and by virtue of and with his unhappiness, I thought. Many people are basically happy because they're up to their necks in unhappiness, I thought, and I told myself that Wertheimer actually was happy because he was continually aware of his unhappiness, could take pleasure in his unhappiness. All at once this thought struck me as not at all absurd, that is to think that he was afraid of losing his unhappiness for a reason I couldn't know and for that reason went to Chur and to Zizers and killed himself. It's possible we have to assume that the so-called unhappy person doesn't exist, I thought, for we first make most of them unhappy by taking *their unhappiness* away from them. Wertheimer was afraid of losing *his unhappiness* and killed himself for this and no other reason, I thought, with a subtle sleight of hand he withdrew from the world, kept a promise so to speak in which no one believed anymore, I thought, withdrew from a world that actually always wanted only to make him and his millions of other suffering companions happy, a condition he however always knew how to prevent with the greatest ruthlessness toward himself and everybody else, because like these others, in deadly fashion, he'd grown more accustomed to his unhappiness than to anything else. After finishing his studies Wertheimer could have given several concerts but he refused, I thought, didn't accept because of Glenn, he was suddenly incapable of playing in public, *just the thought of having to walk on stage makes me ill,* he said, I thought. He received numerous invitations, I thought, and refused all these invitations, he could have gone to Italy, to Hungary, to Czechoslovakia, to Germany, for he had made his mark as they say with the booking agents merely by his evening recitals at the Mozarteum. But everything about him was pure cowardice toward Glenn's triumph with the Goldberg Variations. How can I perform in public now that I've heard Glenn, he often said, while again and again I tried to make him understand that he played better than all the others, *although not as well as Glenn,* which I didn't say to him but which he could intuit in everything I said. The *piano artist,* I said to Wertheimer, and I very often used this notion of the piano artist when speaking to Wertheimer about the art of the piano in order to avoid the repulsive *pianist,* the piano artist then mustn't let himself be so impressed by a genius that he becomes paralyzed, but the fact is you've let yourself be so dazzled by Glenn that you're paralyzed, you, the most extraordinary talent that ever went to the Mozarteum, I said, and I spoke the truth in saying so, for Wertheimer actually was such an extraordinary talent and the Mozarteum has never since seen such an extraordinary talent, even if Wertheimer, as stated, wasn't a genius like Glenn. Don't let yourself be blown over by this Canadian-American whirlwind, I had told Wertheimer, I thought. Those who weren't as extraordinary as Wertheimer didn't let themselves be irritated by Glenn in this lethal fashion, I thought, on the other hand they hadn't recognized the genius Glenn Gould either. Wertheimer had recognized the genius Glenn Gould and was mortally wounded, I thought. And if we wait and refuse the invitations too long, one day we suddenly lack the courage and thus the strength to perform in public, I thought, and Wertheimer, after refusing all invitations for two years after graduating, finally lacked all courage to perform in public, lacked even the strength to answer a booking agency, I thought. What Glenn could manage, that is to decide from one moment to the next never to perform in public again and still continue perfecting himself to the utmost limit of his and basically all piano-instrumental capacities and by isolating himself become the most extraordinary of extraordinary piano artists and finally even the most famous piano artist in the world, naturally wasn't possible for Wertheimer. By avoiding public performances he gradually lost not only his ties with the *concert industry,* as one can rightly call it, but also his musical ability, for Wertheimer was unlike Glenn precisely in the sense that by isolating

himself Glenn could advance his art further and
to the furthest limit, whereas Wertheimer was
more or less ruined by isolating himself. As for
me, I played a few times in Graz and Linz, once
also in Koblenz am Rhein at the invitation of a
student friend, and gave it all up. I no longer took
any pleasure in playing, I didn't intend to prove
myself endlessly before a public, toward which I'd
grown totally indifferent in the meantime and, as
it seemed to me, overnight. Wertheimer however
wasn't at all indifferent toward this public, he suffered from an uninterrupted compulsion, as I have
to call it, to prove himself, as Glenn did by the
way and Glenn perhaps to a much greater degree
than Wertheimer, but Glenn succeeded in doing
what Wertheimer only dreamed about, I thought.
Glenn Gould was the born virtuoso in every respect, I thought, Wertheimer the failure from the
very beginning who couldn't admit his own failure
and all his life couldn't understand it, even though
he was one of our very best piano players, as I can
say without reservation, he was also the typical
failure who failed, who had to fail, at his very first
actual confrontation, that is with Glenn. Glenn
was the genius, Wertheimer nothing but pride, I
thought. Later Wertheimer actually tried to pick
up the pieces, as they say, but he couldn't find the
pieces anymore. Suddenly he was *cut off* from the
art of the piano, I thought. And went, as he himself
repeatedly said, into the so-called human sciences,
without knowing what these human sciences were,
I thought. Came across the science of aphorisms,

that pseudophilosophy, as one might maliciously call it, I thought. Played for years by himself and did nothing but work himself into a state of musical irritability, I thought. Suddenly tried to make his mark as Schopenhauer II, so to speak, or Kant II, Novalis II, filling in this embarrassing pseudophilosophy with Brahms and Handel, with Chopin and Rachmaninoff. And henceforth considered himself repulsive, at least that's the impression I had when I saw him again years later. His Bösendorfer was thenceforth only a source of musical *background* for his work in the human sciences, here's the place for that ugly word, I thought. In two years he lost practically everything; what he'd acquired in twelve years of study, I thought, was no longer audible in his playing, I recall visiting him in Traich twelve or thirteen years ago and being shocked by his *chopstick clinking*, for that's how he played for me in a bout of artistic sentimentality. It struck me as unlikely that by offering to play something for me he had consciously hoped to demonstrate the total decline of his art, I thought rather he hoped I would encourage him, even and especially then, to pursue a career that he'd stopped believing in for nearly a decade, but there was no chance I would encourage him, I told him right out he was washed up, he should keep his hands off the piano, it was embarrassing, nothing else, to have to listen to him, his playing had made me tremendously confused and sad. He snapped the Bösendorfer shut, stood up, went outside, didn't come back for two hours, brooded the whole evening, I thought. The piano had become a dead end for him, the so-called human sciences were no substitute, I thought. Having set out to be great virtuosos, they spend the remaining decades of their existences as piano teachers, I thought, our fellow students in the conservatory now call themselves musical pedagogues and lead a disgusting pedagogical existence, are dependent on talentless students and their megalomaniacal, art-obsessed parents while they dream of music-teacher pension plans inside their petit-bourgeois apartments. Ninety-eight percent of all music conservatory students enroll in our academies with the highest expectations and after graduating spend decades of their lives as so-called music professors in the most absurd fashion, I thought. I, like Wertheimer, was spared that existence, I thought, but also that other lifestyle that I always hated with an equal passion and that leads our well-known and famous piano players from one city to the next and finally from one spa to the next and finally from one provincial hole to the next until their fingers grow lame and their virtuoso senility has taken complete possession of them. When we arrive in such a provincial hole we're sure to see a poster nailed to a tree advertising one of our former fellow students who is playing Mozart, Beethoven and Bartók in the only hall in town, usually it's a shabby hall in an inn somewhere, I thought, and it turns our stomach. We were spared such an ignoble fate, I thought. Out of a thousand piano players only one or two don't go this pitiful, repulsive route, I thought. Today not a single person knows I once studied piano, as one can say, that I attended and graduated from a music conservatory and was actually one of the best piano players in Austria, if not Europe, like Wertheimer, I thought, today I write down this nonsense which I dare tell myself is *essayistic*, to use this hated word once again on my way to self-destruction, I write down these essayistic remarks, which in the end I will have to curse and tear up and thus destroy, and not a single person knows anymore that I myself once played the Goldberg Variations, though not as well as Glenn Gould, whom I've been trying to describe for years because I judge myself to be more qualified than anyone else to write such a description, that I went to the Mozarteum, which is still *considered* one of the premier music conservatories in the whole world, and that I myself have given concerts and not just in Bad Reichenhall and Bad Krozingen, I thought. That I once was a fanatical music student, a fanatical piano virtuoso, who competed on a par with Glenn Gould in playing Brahms and Bach and Schönberg. Whereas personally this secrecy was always to my advantage and thus a great help to me, I thought, this secrecy always profoundly harmed my friend Wertheimer, whereas I have always propped myself up with this secrecy, he was always sickened and made sick by this secrecy, and finally, as I now firmly believe, *killed* by it. For me the fact that I played the piano for fifteen years day and night and because of this practice finally achieved a thoroughly extraordinary degree of perfection was always a weapon not only against my surroundings but also against myself, but Wertheimer always *suffered* from this fact. In everything and anything the fact of my piano study has always been useful for me, I mean it has been crucial, and precisely because no one knows anything about it, precisely because it's forgotten and because I keep it secret. For Wertheimer however this same fact has always been the root of his unhappiness, of his uninterrupted existential depression, I thought. I was much better than most of the others in the Academy, I thought, I *stopped* from one moment to the next, that strengthened me, made me stronger than those, I thought, who didn't stop and who weren't better than me and who took lifelong refuge in their amateurishness, call themselves professors and let themselves be decorated with titles and medals, I thought. All these musical idiots who graduated from our conservatories and went into the concert business, as they say, I thought. I never went into the concert business, I thought, something inside me wouldn't allow it, but I didn't go into the concert business for a completely other reason than Wertheimer, who, as mentioned, didn't go into it because of Glenn Gould or at least broke it off immediately, as they say, because of Glenn Gould, something inside me wouldn't let me go into the concert business, whereas Wertheimer's path was blocked by Glenn Gould. A concertistic life is the most horrible imaginable, no matter whose, it's awful to play the piano before an audience, not to mention the awfulness of having to sing before an audience, I thought. It's our greatest fortune to be able to say we studied at a famous conservatory and graduated from this famous conservatory, as they say, and do nothing with it and keep the whole thing a secret, I thought. Don't piss away this fortune by performing in public for years and decades, etc., I thought, but consider the whole thing a closed book in order to keep it a secret. But I've always been a genius of secrecy, I thought, quite unlike Wertheimer who basically couldn't keep anything a secret, had to talk about everything, had to get everything out in the open as long as he lived. But naturally unlike most others we were lucky not to have to earn a cent because we had enough from the very beginning. Whereas Wertheimer was always ashamed of this money, I myself was never ashamed of this money, I thought, for it would have been crazy to be ashamed of the money one was born into, at least I think it would have been perverse, in any case disgustingly hypocritical, I thought. Everywhere we look we find hypocrites claiming to be ashamed of the money they have and that others don't have, whereas it's in the nature of things that some people have money and the others have none, and sometimes they have no money and the others have some and vice versa, nothing will change there, and there's no reason to feel guilty about having money, just as there's none to feel guilty about not having it, etc., I thought, a fact which

nobody understands however, neither the haves
nor the have-nots, because in the end the only
thing they understand is hypocrisy and nothing
else. I never reproached myself for having money,
I thought, Wertheimer constantly reproached
himself for it, I never said I suffered from being
wealthy, unlike Wertheimer, who said it very
often and who didn't shy away from the most
inane spending maneuvers, which in the end didn't
help him at all, the millions he sent for example
to the Sahel region in Africa and that, as he later
learned, never arrived because they were gobbled
up by the Catholic organizations he entrusted the
money to. The uncertainty of man is his nature,
is his desperation, as Wertheimer very often and
very correctly put it, it's just that he never managed
to hold himself to his own observations, to hold
fast to them, he always had monstrous, truly monstrous *theories* spinning around in his head (and
in his aphorisms!), I thought, actually a redemp-
tive philosophy for life and human existence, but
he was incapable of applying it to himself. In theory he mastered all the unpleasantness of life, all
degrees of desperation, the evil in the world that
grinds us down, *but in practice he was never up
to it*. And so he went to pot, completely at odds
with his own theories, went all the way to suicide,
I thought, all the way to Zizers, his ridiculous end
of the line, I thought. In theory he had always
spoken out against suicide, deemed *me* capable of
it however without a second thought, always went
to *my* funeral, in practice *he* killed himself and *I*

went to *his* funeral. In theory he became one of the greatest piano virtuosos in the world, one of the most famous artists of all time (even if not as famous as Glenn Gould!), in practice he accomplished nothing at the piano, I thought, and fled in the most pitiful manner into his so-called human sciences. In theory he was a master of existence, in practice he not only didn't master his existence but was destroyed by it, I thought. In theory he was our friend, that is my friend and Glenn's, in practice he never was, I thought, for he lacked everything necessary for *actual* friendship, as he did for musical virtuosity, as his suicide indicates, I thought. The so-called bottom line is *he* killed himself, not *I*, I thought, I was just picking up my suitcase from the floor to put it on the bench, when the innkeeper walked in. She was surprised, she said, hadn't heard me, I thought, she's lying to me. She surely saw me enter the inn, has been spying on me the whole time, hasn't come into the restaurant on purpose, that disgusting, repulsive and yet seductive creature, who's left her blouse open to the waist. The vulgarity of these people who don't even try to hide it, I thought, who put their vulgarity on display, I thought. Who don't need to hide their vulgarity, their commonness, I said to myself. The room I always stayed in, she said, wasn't heated, but it probably wouldn't be necessary to turn on the heat since it was warm outside, she would open the windows in the room and let in the warm spring air, she said, while starting to button up her blouse without actually

buttoning up the blouse. Wertheimer had been
with her, she said, before he left for Zizers. That
he had killed himself she learned from the transporter, the transporter had heard it from one of
the woodsmen who looked after and guarded
Wertheimer's property, from Kohlroser (Franz).
It wasn't clear who would take over Traich, she
said, Wertheimer's sister surely wouldn't, she
thought, she was in Switzerland for good. She had
seen her only twice in the last ten years, an *un-
approachable woman*, completely different from
her brother who was approachable, she even used
the word *affable*, which surprised me, since I had
never connected the word affable with Wertheimer. Wertheimer had been *good* to everyone, she
said, she actually said *good*, but in the same breath
said he had *abandoned* Traich. Recently outsiders
had often shown up in Traich, stayed for days and
even weeks, without Wertheimer himself putting
in an appearance in Traich, people who had gotten
the key to Traich from Wertheimer, as she said,
artists, musicians, her tone of voice in saying the
words *artists* and *musicians* was contemptuous.
These people, she said, had only exploited Wertheimer and his house in Traich, drank and ate for
days and weeks at his expense, lolled around in
bed until noon, traipsed through town laughing
loudly and in crazy clothes, all of them disheveled,
in her opinion they had made the worst impression. One could see that Wertheimer himself, she
claimed, was getting more and more disheveled,
she drew out the word *disheveled*, she got that

from Wertheimer, I thought. In the night she would hear Wertheimer play the piano, she said, often half the night until morning, finally he would walk through town with bags under his eyes, his clothing wrinkled and torn, would come into her inn for no other purpose than to *have a good sleep*. In the last months he stopped going to Vienna, wasn't even interested in the mail waiting for him there, hadn't had this mail forwarded. For four months he was alone in Traich without leaving the house, the woodsmen brought him supplies, as she said while picking up my suitcase and going up to my room. Immediately she opened the window and said that no one else had spent the night in this room for the whole winter, everything was dirty, she said, if I didn't mind she would get a rag and clean things up, at least the soot on the windowsill, she said, but I refused, I couldn't care less about the dirt. She turned down the covers and claimed the sheets were clean, the air would dry them. Every guest always wants the same room, she said. Wertheimer never used to let anyone spend the night in Traich, all at once his house was teeming with people, the innkeeper said. For thirty years no one besides Wertheimer had spent the night in Traich, in the last weeks before his death dozens of city people, as she put it, had stopped in Traich, spent the night in Traich, *turned* the whole house *upside down*, she said. These artists, she said, were *peculiar* types, the word *peculiar* wasn't hers either, she got it from Wertheimer who was fond of the word *peculiar*, as I thought. For a long time people like Wertheimer (and me!) put up with their isolation, I thought, then they have to have company, for twenty years Wertheimer held out without company, then he filled his house with all sorts of people. And killed himself, I thought. Like my house in Desselbrunn, Traich is meant for solitude, I thought, for someone like me, like Wertheimer, I thought, for an artist type, a so-called intellectual type, but if we push a house like this one beyond a very specific limit it kills us, it's absolutely lethal. At first we equip a house like this one for our artistic and intellectual purposes, and once we've equipped it, it kills us, I thought, the way the innkeeper wipes the dirt from the wardrobe door with her bare fingers, completely without embarrassment, on the contrary she enjoyed the fact that I watched her do it, that I kept my eyes on her so to speak. Now I suddenly understood why Wertheimer had slept with her. I said I would probably spend only one night at the inn, I'd suddenly felt the need to visit Traich one more time and thus spend the night in her inn, did she recall the name Glenn Gould, I asked her, yes, she answered, *the world-famous one*. He made it past fifty like Wertheimer, I said, the piano virtuoso, the best in the whole world, who was once in Traich twenty-eight years ago, I said, which she probably didn't recall but she immediately contradicted this by saying she distinctly recalled *this American*. But this Glenn Gould didn't kill himself, I said, he had a stroke, *fell over dead at the piano*, I said, I was conscious of the helplessness with which I said it, but I was less embarrassed before the innkeeper than before myself, I heard myself say *fell over dead* again as the innkeeper went to the open window to confirm that the stench from the paper factory was fouling the air, as it always did in windy weather, she said. Wertheimer killed himself, I said, *this Glenn Gould* didn't, he died a natural death, I've never said anything so stilted in my life, I thought. Perhaps Wertheimer killed himself because *this Glenn Gould* had died. A stroke was a wonderful way to go, said the innkeeper, everybody wants to have a stroke, a fatal one. A sudden end. I'm going to Traich immediately, I said, did the innkeeper know whether someone was in Traich, who was guarding the house now. She didn't know, but surely the woodsmen were in Traich. In her opinion nothing had changed in Traich since Wertheimer's death. Wertheimer's sister, who without doubt had inherited Traich, hadn't even put in an appearance here, *nor had any other heir*, as she said. Whether I cared to eat something that evening in her inn, she asked, I said I couldn't say now what I would want this evening, naturally I would eat one of her sausage and onion salads, I can't get them anywhere else, I thought, but I didn't say that, I only thought it. Business was as usual, the workers in the paper factory kept it going, they all came in the evening, hardly ever for lunch, that's the way it always was. If anybody, it was the beer-truck drivers and woodsmen who came to the restaurant for some liverwurst, she said. But she had enough to do. That she was once married to a paper worker, I thought, whom she lived with for three years until he fell into one of the dreaded paper mills and was ground to death by this paper mill, and that she never married afterward. My husband has been dead for nine years, she said spontaneously, and sat down on the bench by the window. Marriage was out of the question now, she said, it's better to be alone. But at first you risk everything for it, to get married, to find a husband; she didn't say, and then I was happy he was gone, which she certainly was thinking, she said the accident didn't have to happen, *Herr Wertheimer was a great help to me in the period after the funeral.* The moment she couldn't stand living with her husband, I thought while watching her, he fell into the paper mill and was gone, left her at least a proper, if not sufficient, pension. *My husband was a good person,* she said, *you knew him of course,* although I could barely remember this husband, only that he always wore the same felt overalls from the paper factory, sat at a table in the restaurant with a felt cap from the paper factory on his head, putting away tremendous quantities of smoked meat that his wife placed in front of him. *My husband was a good man,* she repeated several times, looking out the window and straightening her hair. Being alone also has its advantages, she said. I had surely been at the funeral, she said and instantly wanted to know everything about Wertheimer's funeral, she already knew it had taken place in Chur, but she wasn't familiar with the immediate circumstances that had led to Wertheimer's funeral, and so I sat down on the bed and gave a report. Naturally I could only give her a fragmentary report, I started by saying I'd been in Vienna, occupied with the sale of my apartment, a large apartment I said, much too big for one person and completely unnecessary for someone who has taken up residence in Madrid, that most wonderful of cities, I said. But I didn't sell the apartment, I said, just as I have no intention of selling Desselbrunn, which she knew. For she once visited Desselbrunn with her husband, many years ago, *when the dairy farm burned down,* I said, with the economic crisis we have today it would be crazy to sell a piece of realty, I said, purposely repeating the word *realty* several times, it was crucial for my report. The state is bankrupt, I said, at that she shook her head, the government is sleazy, I said, the socialists who have been in power now for almost thirteen years have exploited their power to the hilt and completely ruined the state. As I spoke the innkeeper nodded her head, alternately looking at me and out the window. They all wanted a socialist government, I said, but now they see that precisely this socialist government has squandered everything, I purposely pronounced the word *squandered* more clearly than all the others, I wasn't even ashamed of having used it at all, I repeated the word *squandered* a few more times with regard to our bankrupt state and our socialist government, adding that our chancellor was a low-down, cunning, shady character who had simply exploited socialism as a vehicle for his perverse power trips, like the whole government by the way, I said, all these politicians are nothing but power-hungry, unscrupulous, vulgar schemers, the state, which they themselves constitute, is everything to them, I said, the people they represent mean just about nothing to them. I am and love this people, but I won't have anything to do with this state, I said. *Never before in its history* has our country sunk so low, I said, never before in its history has it been governed by more vulgar and therefore more spineless cretins. But the people are stupid, I said, and are too weak to change such a situation, they are always taken in by untrustworthy, power-hungry people like the ones in government today. Probably nothing about this situation will change in the next elections, I said, for Austrians are creatures of habit and they've even grown accustomed to the muck they've been wading in for the last ten years. These pitiful people, I said. Austrians especially are always taken in by the word *socialism*, I said, although everyone knows that the word *socialism* has lost all meaning. Our socialists aren't socialists anymore, I said, today's socialists are the new capitalists, all a sham, I said to the innkeeper, who however didn't want to listen to my senseless digression, as I suddenly noticed, for she was still thirsting for my funeral report. And so I said I had been surprised in Vienna by a telegram from Zizers, a telegram from the Duttweiler woman, I said, Wertheimer's sister, reached me in Vienna, I was in the famous Palm House, I said, and found the telegram at the door. To this day I'm not sure how this Frau Duttweiler knew I was in Vienna, I said. A city that has grown ugly, which can't be compared with the Vienna that used to be. A terrible experience, after years abroad, to come back to this city, to this decadent country, I said. That Wertheimer's sister telegraphed me at all, that she informed me of her brother's death at all, came as a surprise, I said. Duttweiler, I said, what an awful name! A rich Swiss family, I said, which Wertheimer's sister had married into, a chemical plant. But as she herself knew, I said to the innkeeper, Wertheimer always oppressed his sister, wouldn't leave her alone, at the last, the very last possible moment, she pulled away from him. If the innkeeper were to go to Vienna, I said, she'd be horrified. How this city has changed for the worst, I said. No trace of grandeur, all scum! I said. The best thing is to keep out of everything, withdraw from everything, I said. Not for a second have I regretted going away to Madrid years ago. But if we don't have the chance to go away and have to stay in such a cretinous country, in such a cretinous city as Vienna, we perish, we don't hold out for long, I said. In Vienna I had two days to think about Wertheimer, I said, on the train to Chur, during the night before the funeral. How many people had been at Wertheimer's funeral, she wanted to know. Only the Duttweiler woman, her husband and I, I said. And of course the undertakers, I said. Everything was over in less than twenty minutes. The innkeeper said Wertheimer had always told her that should he die before her, he would leave her a necklace, *a valuable one*, she said, *from his grandmother*. But Wertheimer surely wouldn't have mentioned her in his will, she claimed, and I thought that Wertheimer certainly hadn't even made a will. If Wertheimer promised the innkeeper a necklace, I said to her, she'll get this necklace. Wertheimer had spent the night in her inn from time to time, she said with a red face, when he was frightened in Traich, as he often was, upon arriving from Vienna he would first go to her inn to spend the night, for he came to Traich from Vienna during the winter surprisingly often and there was no heat in Traich. The people he'd invited to Traich recently wore *wild clothing, actors*, she said, *like circus people*. They never drank or ate in her inn, stocked up on all sorts of drinks from the general store. They just used him, the innkeeper said, hung out for weeks in Traich at his expense, made a mess of everything, made noise the whole night until morning. *What trash*, she said. For weeks they'd been in Traich on their own, without Wertheimer, who showed up only a few days before his trip to Chur. Wertheimer often told the innkeeper that he was going to visit his sister and his brother-in-law in Zizers but kept putting it off. He sent many letters to his sister in Zizers, she should come back to him in Traich, separate from her husband for whom he, Wertheimer, had never had any respect, as the innkeeper said, *for this dreadful person*, as she said with Wertheimer's words, but his sister hadn't answered his letters. We can't tie a person to us, I said, if a person doesn't want it we have to leave him alone, I thought. Wertheimer had wanted to tie his sister to him for all eternity, I said, that was a mistake. He drove his sister crazy and in the process went mad himself, I said, for it's madness to kill yourself. What will happen now to all the money Wertheimer left behind? the innkeeper asked. I didn't know, I said, his sister had surely inherited it, I thought. *Money goes to money*, the innkeeper said, then she wanted to know more about the funeral, but I didn't know what else to report, I had already said everything about Wertheimer's funeral, more or less everything. Was it a *Jewish funeral*, the innkeeper wanted to know. I said, *no, no Jewish funeral*, he was buried the fastest way possible, I said, everything went so fast I almost missed it. The Duttweilers invited me to a meal after the funeral, I said, but I refused, I didn't want to be with them. But that was a mistake, I said, I should have accepted and had lunch with them, as a result I was suddenly standing there alone and didn't know what to do, I said. Chur is an ugly city, I said, gloomy like no other. Wertheimer was only buried *provisionally* in Chur, I suddenly said, they want to bury him *permanently in Vienna*, in the Döbling cemetery, I said, in the family crypt. The innkeeper stood up and claimed that the mild air outside would warm up my room before evening, I could rest assured. The winter cold is still in these rooms, she said. At the thought of having to spend the night in this room, where I had already spent so many sleepless nights, I actually became afraid of catching cold. I couldn't have gone anywhere else however, because either it was too far or was even more primitive than here, I thought. Of course I was once much less demanding, I thought, not yet as sensitive as I am today, and I thought that in any event I would ask the innkeeper for two wool blankets before I went to bed. Whether she could make me some hot tea before I went to Traich, I asked the innkeeper, who then went down to the kitchen to make some hot tea. In the meantime I unpacked my bag, opened the wardrobe and hung up the dark gray suit I had taken along to Chur as my funeral suit, so to speak. Everywhere they hang these tacky Raphael angels in their rooms, I thought while looking at the Raphael angel on the wall, which had already become moldy but for that reason was now bearable. I recalled that I'd been wakened around five in the morning by the sound of pigs bumping against the trough, of the innkeeper thoughtlessly and stupidly closing the door. When we know what's in store for us, I thought, it's easier to deal with it. I bent down to see myself in the mirror and discovered that the infection on my temple, which I'd been treating for weeks with a Chinese ointment and which had gone away, was now suddenly back, this observation made me anxious. I immediately thought of a nasty disease that my doctor was concealing from me and that, simply to humor me, he was treating with this Chinese ointment, which in truth, as I now had to conclude, was worthless. Such an infection can naturally be the start of a severe, nasty disease, I thought and turned around. That I had gotten out in Attnang-Puchheim and traveled to Wankham in order to get to Traich suddenly struck me as totally senseless. I could have done without this dreadful Wankham, I thought, I didn't need that, I thought, suddenly to be standing in this cold, musty room, afraid of the night, all of whose horrors I had no trouble imagining. To have stayed in Vienna and not responded to this Duttweiler woman's telegram and not gone to Chur, I said to myself, would have been better than embarking on this trip to Chur, getting out in Attnang-Puchheim and going to Wankham to see Traich one more time, which is none of my business. Since I hadn't said a word to the Duttweilers and even at Wertheimer's open grave didn't feel the slightest pang of emotion, I thought, I might as well have spared myself the whole agony, not taken the trip upon myself. My behavior disgusted me. On the other hand, what would I have had to discuss with Wertheimer's sister? I asked myself. With her husband, whom I had nothing to do with and who actually repelled me, even more in my personal encounter with him than in Wertheimer's descriptions, which of course had put him in a worse than unfavorable light. I make it a point not to speak with people like the Duttweilers, I thought at once

upon seeing Duttweiler. But even a man like Duttweiler was able to make Wertheimer's sister leave
her brother and move to Switzerland, I thought,
even a man as repulsive as Duttweiler! I looked in
the mirror again and observed that the infection
was not just on my right temple but had already
reached the back of my head. It's possible the
Duttweiler woman will go back to Vienna now, I
thought, her brother is dead, the Kohlmarkt apartment has been vacated for her, she no longer needs
Switzerland. The Vienna apartment belongs to her,
Traich as well. On top of which it's her furniture
in the Kohlmarkt apartment, I thought, which she
loved, which her brother, as he himself always
said, hated. Now she can live in peace with her
Swiss husband in Zizers, I thought, for at any time
she can move back to Vienna or Traich. The virtuoso lies in the Chur cemetery near the garbage
heap, I thought for a moment. Wertheimer's parents had been buried according to Jewish rites, I
thought, Wertheimer himself had always characterized himself as *agnostic*. With Wertheimer I had
visited the Wertheimer crypt in the Döbling cemetery, right next to the so-called Lieben crypt and
the Theodor Herzl grave, it hadn't irritated him
that a beech tree growing out of the crypt had
progressively dislodged the immense granite block
inscribed with the names of all the Wertheimers
in the Wertheimer crypt; his sister had always
wanted to make him cut down the beech tree and
put the granite block back in place, the fact that
the beech tree had shot up out of the crypt and

dislodged the granite block didn't disturb him, on the contrary, every time he visited the crypt he marveled at the beech tree and the increasingly dislodged granite block. Now his sister will have the beech tree removed from the crypt and the granite block set straight and before that she will have Wertheimer *transported* from Chur to Vienna and buried in the crypt, I thought. Wertheimer was the most passionate cemetery lover I have ever known, even more passionate than me, I thought. With my right index finger I drew a large *W* on the dusty wardrobe door. Desselbrunn came to my mind at this point, for a moment I caught myself in the sentimental thought of perhaps also going to Desselbrunn, but repressed this thought immediately. I wanted to stick to my principles and said to myself, I'm not going to Desselbrunn, I'm not going to Desselbrunn for the next five or six years. Such a visit to Desselbrunn will surely weaken me for years, I said to myself, I can't afford a Desselbrunn visit. The countryside outside my window was the dreary, sickening countryside I knew so well from Desselbrunn and which years ago I suddenly couldn't take anymore. If I hadn't left Desselbrunn, I said to myself, I would have succumbed, I wouldn't be here anymore, I would have succumbed *before* Glenn and *before* Wertheimer, wasted away, as I have to say, for the countryside around Desselbrunn is a countryside meant for wasting away, like the countryside outside this window in Wankham, which threatens everybody, slowly suffocates everybody, never uplifts, never protects. We're not asked to choose our place of birth, I thought. But we can leave our place of birth if it threatens to suffocate us, go off and away from the place that will kill us if we miss the moment of going off and away. I was lucky and left at the right moment, I said to myself. And in the end left Vienna, because Vienna was threatening to suffocate and choke me. Nevertheless I owe it to my father's bank account that I'm still alive, still *am allowed* to exist, as I suddenly said to myself. Not a life-giving region, I said to myself. Not a soothing countryside. Not pleasant people. Lying in wait for me, I thought. Making me anxious. Pulling the wool over my eyes. I've never felt safe in this region, I thought. Constantly visited by disease, almost killed finally by insomnia. Sigh of relief when the men from Altmünster came and took away the Steinway, I thought, sudden freedom of movement in Desselbrunn. Didn't give up art and whatever else the term means by giving the Steinway to the schoolteacher's child in Altmünster, I thought. To have exposed the Steinway to a schoolteacher's vulgarity, exposed it to the cretinism of the schoolteacher's child. If I'd told the schoolteacher what my Steinway was truly worth he would have been shocked, I thought, this way he had no idea of the instrument's value. Even when I had the Steinway transported from Vienna to Desselbrunn I knew it wouldn't be in Desselbrunn for long, but naturally I had no idea I would give it away to the schoolteacher's child, I thought. As long as I had the Steinway I wasn't independent in my writing, I thought, wasn't free, as I was from the moment the Steinway was out of the house for good. I had to part with the Steinway in order to write, to be honest I had been writing for fourteen years and actually had only written more or less useless junk because I hadn't parted with my Steinway. The Steinway was barely out the door and I was writing better, I thought. In the Calle del Prado I was always thinking about the Steinway standing in Vienna (or in Desselbrunn) and thus could write nothing better than these inevitably botched attempts. I'd barely gotten rid of the Steinway and I was writing differently, from the first moment, I thought. But that doesn't mean of course that I'd given up music with the Steinway, I thought. On the contrary. But it no longer had the same devastating power over me, simply didn't hurt me anymore, I thought. When we peer into this countryside we are frightened. Under no circumstances do we want to return to this countryside. Everything is perpetually gray and the people are always depressing. Then I would just crawl into my room and be incapable of thinking a single useful thought, I thought. And would gradually become like everybody here, I just need to look at the innkeeper, this person who has been totally destroyed by the all-governing force of nature here, who can't get out of her petty, vulgar ways, I thought. I would have perished in this evil-spirited countryside. But I never should have gone to Desselbrunn, I thought, never should have accepted my inheritance, could have renounced it, *now I've abandoned it*, I thought. Desselbrunn was originally built by one of my great-uncles, who was director of the paper factory, as a manor house with rooms for all his many children. Simply abandoned it, that was my salvation, surely. At first went to Desselbrunn with my parents only in the summer, then went to school for years in Desselbrunn and in Wankham, I thought, then to the gymnasium in Salzburg, then to the Mozarteum, once also for a year to the Vienna Academy, I thought, back to the Mozarteum, then back to Vienna and finally to Desselbrunn with the idea of withdrawing there permanently with my intellectual ambitions, but where I very quickly succumbed to the realization that I'd wound up in a dead end. The piano virtuoso career as an escape, but pushed nonetheless to the most extreme limit, to perfection, I thought. At the height of my ability, as I can say, gave everything up, *tossed it out the window*, as I *have* to say, hit myself on the head, gave away the Steinway. When it rains here for six or seven weeks without stopping and the local inhabitants go crazy in this unstoppable rain, I thought, one has to have tremendous discipline not to kill oneself. But half the people here kill themselves sooner or later, don't die a natural death, as one says. Have nothing but their Catholicism and the Socialist Party, the two most disgusting institutions of our time. In Madrid I leave the house at least once a day to eat, I thought, here I would never have left the house in my increasingly hopeless deterioration process. But I never seriously thought about selling, I toyed with the idea, as in the last two years, sure, but naturally without results. At the same time I never promised anyone responsible for such things *not* to sell Desselbrunn, I thought. No sale is possible without real estate agents and I shudder at the idea of real estate agents, I thought. We can leave a house like Desselbrunn standing for years without a problem, I thought, let it go to seed, I thought, why not. I won't go to Desselbrunn under any circumstances, I thought. The innkeeper had made me my tea and I went down to the restaurant. I sat at the table by the window where I used to sit in past years, but it didn't seem to me that time had stood still. I heard the innkeeper working in the kitchen and I thought she was probably making lunch for her child who came home from school at one or two, warming up some goulash or perhaps some vegetable soup. In theory we understand people, but in practice we can't put up with them, I thought, deal with them for the most part reluctantly and always treat them from our own point of view. We should observe and treat people not from our point of view but from all angles, I thought, associate with them in such a way that we can say we associate with them so to speak in a completely unbiased way, which however isn't possible, since we actually are always biased against everybody. The innkeeper once had a lung disease like mine, I thought, like me she was able to squeeze this lung illness out of her, liquidate it with her will to live. She finished high school by the skin of her teeth, as they say, I thought, and then took over the inn from her uncle, who had been implicated in a murder case that even today hasn't been entirely cleared up and who was sentenced to twenty years in prison. Together with a neighbor, her uncle is said to have strangled a so-called *haberdashery* salesman from Vienna who had stopped for the night, strangled him in the room next to mine to get at the enormous sum of money that the Viennese salesman is said to have had with him. The *Dichtel Mill*, as the inn is called, has been so to speak notorious since this murder case. At first, that is when the murder case became known, the Dichtel Mill started going downhill and was closed for more than two years. The court turned over ownership of the Dichtel Mill to the niece of the murderer, that is her uncle, the niece took over the Dichtel Mill and reopened it, but naturally since the reopening it was no longer the same Dichtel Mill it was before the murder. No one ever heard anything more about the innkeeper's uncle, I thought, but he probably was let out after just twelve or thirteen years, like all murderers and criminals sentenced to twenty years, it's also possible he's no longer alive, I thought, I wasn't planning to ask the innkeeper for news about her uncle for I had no desire to hear the murder story, which she had already told me several times and once more at my request, from the beginning. The murder of the Viennese salesman had caused a sensation back then, and during the trial the daily newspapers spoke of nothing else and the Dichtel Mill, long boarded up, was besieged by curious visitors for weeks, although there was nothing particularly worth seeing at the Dichtel Mill. Since the murder case the Dichtel Mill has always been called the *murder house*, and when people want to say they're going *to the Dichtel Mill* they also say they're going *to the murder house*, it's become a local tradition. At the trial the prosecutor presented only circumstantial evidence, I thought, and the murder wasn't actually traced to the innkeeper's uncle or his accomplice, whose family was plunged into misfortune, as they say, by the whole murder story. Even the court had trouble believing the so-called path-clearer capable of committing such a murder in concert with the innkeeper's uncle, who was known everywhere and by everybody as *easygoing and modest and a solid citizen through and through* and even today is considered easygoing and modest and a solid citizen by those who knew him, but the jurors decided on the maximum sentence, and not just for the innkeeper's uncle but also for the former path-clearer, who, as I know, died in the meantime, as his wife always said, of grief at having been the innocent victim of misanthropic jurors. The courts, even after they have destroyed innocent people and their families for life, go back to their everyday business, I thought, the jurors, who always follow the mere whim of a moment in their judgment, but also a boundless hatred for their fellowman, will quickly come to terms with their mistake and themselves even after they have long since recognized that they've committed an irreparable crime against innocent people. Half of all convictions, I have heard it said, actually rest on such mistaken verdicts, I thought, and it's a hundred to one that the so-called *Dichtel Mill trial* was just like the others, that the jurors reached a mistaken verdict. The so-called Austrian municipal courts are known for the fact that every year dozens of mistaken verdicts are reached by jurors who thus have dozens of innocent people on their conscience, most of whom are serving a life sentence in our correctional institutions without the prospect of ever being *rehabilitated*, as they say. In fact, I thought, there are more innocent than guilty people in our prisons and correctional institutions because there are so many conscienceless judges and misanthropic jurors who despise their fellowman, who take revenge for their own unhappiness and their own hideousness on those who, because of the horrifying circumstances that have led them into court, are at their mercy. The Austrian criminal system is diabolical, I thought, as we repeatedly are forced to conclude if we read the newspapers carefully, but it becomes even more diabolical when we know that only the tiniest portion of its crimes comes to light and is made public. Personally I'm convinced that the innkeeper's uncle was not the murderer or rather the murderer's accomplice that he was branded as thirteen or fourteen years ago, I thought. I also judge the path-clearer to actually be innocent, I still recall the trial reports in detail and at bottom both of them, the innkeeper's uncle, the so-called Dichtel-keeper, as well as his neighbor the path-clearer, absolutely should have been exonerated, in the end even the prosecutor pleaded for that, the jurors however convicted them both of first-degree homicide and had the Dichtel-keeper and the path-clearer carted off to the Garsten prison, I thought. And if no one has the courage and the strength and the money to reopen such a ghastly case, as they say, a mistaken verdict like that of the Dichtel-keeper and the path-clearer simply stands, such a ghastly miscarriage of justice against two truly innocent people whom one, and that means society, finally wants to have nothing to do with for all time, whether guilty or innocent, it doesn't matter. The Dichtel Mill trial, as it was always called, came to my mind and kept me occupied the whole time I sat at the window table because I'd discovered the photograph tacked to the wall facing me, a photograph that showed the Dichtel-keeper in his innkeeper coat, smoking a pipe, and I thought that the innkeeper probably nailed the photograph to the wall not only out of gratitude to her uncle who had given her the Dichtel Mill and provided her with her livelihood but also to keep the Dichtel miller or rather the Dichtel-keeper from being completely forgotten. But most of the people who were truly and actively interested in the Dichtel Mill trial have long since died, I thought, and people today can't understand the photograph. But it's true that a certain odor of felony still clings to the Dichtel Mill, I thought,

which naturally attracts people. We're not unhappy when people become suspects and are
charged with a crime and locked up, I thought,
that's the truth. When crimes come to light, I
thought while looking at the photograph opposite
me. When she comes back from the kitchen I'll
ask the innkeeper what has become of her uncle,
I thought, and I said to myself, I'll ask her about
it, then I said, I won't ask her about it, I'll ask
her, I won't ask her, in this way I kept staring at
the photograph of the Dichtel-keeper the whole
time and thought, I'll ask the innkeeper all about
him, etc. Suddenly a so-called simple person, who
of course is never a simple person, is ripped out
of his surroundings, actually put in prison at the
drop of a hat, I thought, from which he can only
emerge, if he emerges at all, as a totally destroyed
human being, as legal flotsam and jetsam, as I had
to say to myself, for which finally all society is
responsible. After the trial was over the newspapers debated the question whether the Dichtel-
keeper as well as the path-clearer might actually
be innocent and wrote editorials to this effect, but
two, three days after the trial was over no one
talked about the Dichtel Mill trial. From these
editorials one could deduce that the two who were
branded and sentenced as murderers *couldn't* have
committed the murder, a third party or several
third parties must have committed the murder, but
of course the jurors had already reached their verdict and the trial was never reopened, I thought,
in my life few things have actually absorbed me

with greater intensity than the criminal-justice aspect of our world. When we follow this criminal-justice aspect of our world, and that means of our society, we experience miracles, as they say, on a daily basis. When the innkeeper came out of the kitchen and sat down at my table, more or less exhausted, she had been washing clothes and reeked of kitchen odors, I asked her what had become of her uncle, the Dichtel-keeper, putting the question not in a blunt but in an extremely cautious way. Her uncle had moved in with his brother in Hirschbach, she said, Hirschbach was a small town on the Czech border, she herself had been there only once, but that was years ago, her son was just three years old at the time. She'd been planning to show her son to her uncle in the hope that he, who she assumed was still quite rich, would help her through her difficulty, that is give her money, that's the only reason she and her son had undertaken such a grueling trip, to Hirschbach on the Czech border, six months after the death of her husband, the father of her son, who despite all adverse circumstances had turned out so well. But her uncle wouldn't see them, had his brother deny he was there, hadn't shown himself at all until she finally gave up waiting for him with her son and they took the train back to Wankham, empty-handed. How can a person have such a heart of stone, she said, on the other hand, however, she could understand her uncle. He didn't want to hear anything about the Dichtel Mill and Wankham, she said. Prisoners, once they're released, never go back to the place where they were before going to prison, I said. The innkeeper had hoped to get financial help from her uncle or at least from her second uncle, the so-called Hirschbach uncle, but hadn't received this help from precisely the two persons who were her only relatives and today still are and about whom she knew that they, although still living in the meager circumstances she had noted in Hirschbach, disposed of a rather large fortune. The innkeeper also made an allusion to the amount of her two uncles' fortune, without mentioning a definite sum, a pitifully small sum, I thought, but one that must have struck her, the innkeeper, as so enormous that she could see in it the key to her salvation, I thought. Old people, even when they no longer need anything, are stingy, the older they get the stingier they get, won't part with anything, their offspring can starve to death before their eyes and it won't bother them in the slightest. Then the innkeeper described her Hirschbach trip, how tiring it is to go from Wankham to Hirschbach, she'd had to change trains three times with her sick child and her Hirschbach visit not only didn't bring her any money but also gave her a throat infection, a nasty throat infection that lasted for months, as she said. After her visit in Hirschbach she thought she would take down the photograph of her uncle, but then she didn't remove it from the wall because of her customers, who surely would've asked why she'd taken the photograph off the wall, she didn't want to explain the whole story again to everybody, she said. Then they suddenly would've wanted to know everything about the trial, she said, she wouldn't let herself get into that. The fact is she loved her uncle in the photograph *before* the Hirschbach trip, whereas *after* her return from Hirschbach she could only hate him. She had the greatest compassion for him, he not the least for her. Finally *she* started running the Dichtel Mill again as an inn, she said, under the most unfavorable circumstances, she hadn't let the building get run down, hadn't sold it either, although she'd had more than a few offers. Her husband didn't care about the inn business, she explained, she met him at a carnival party in Regau, where she'd gone to buy a few old chairs for her inn that an inn in Regau had thrown out. She saw right away that a good-natured man was sitting there completely alone, without companions. She sat down at his table and took him back to Wankham, where he then stayed. But he never was an innkeeper, she said. Here all married women, she actually used the words *married women*, have to count on their husbands falling into the paper mill, or at least on their having one of their hands or several fingers ripped off by the paper mill, she said, basically it's an everyday event when they injure themselves at the paper mills, and the whole area is filled with men like that who've been crippled by the paper mills. Ninety percent of the men in this town work in the paper factory, she said. No one here has any other plan for their children than to send them right back to the factory, she said, for generations the same mechanism, I thought. And if the paper factory goes broke, she said, they'll all be left high and dry. It was only a matter of the shortest time before the paper factory would close, she explained, everything points that way, since the paper factory has been nationalized it would soon have to close, because like all other nationalized companies it was up to its ears in debt. Here everything revolves around the paper factory, and when it closes everything's over. She herself would be washed up, for ninety percent of her customers worked in the factory, she said, paper workers at least spend their money, she explained, woodsmen on the other hand not at all, and farmers would turn up in her inn once or twice a year, they also had stayed clear of the Dichtel Mill since the days of the trial, wouldn't come in without asking unpleasant questions, so she said. She had long since stopped worrying about this hopeless future, it didn't matter what would happen to her, after all her son was twelve now and at fourteen the kids around here can already stand on their own two feet. I'm not the least bit interested in my future, she said. That Herr Wertheimer, as she put it, had always been *a welcome guest* in her inn. But *such refined gentlemen* have no idea what it means to live the way she does, to run an inn like the Dichtel Mill. They (the refined gentlemen) always talked about matters she didn't understand, didn't have any worries and spent all their time thinking about what they should do with their money and their time. She herself had never had enough money and never enough time and hadn't even been unhappy once, in contrast to those she called *refined gentlemen*, who always had enough money and enough time and constantly talked about their unhappiness. She was totally incapable of understanding how Wertheimer could always tell her he was an unhappy person. Often he sat in the restaurant until one in the morning, bemoaning his fate, and she *took pity* on him, as she said, took him up to her room because he no longer wanted to go back to Traich at night. That people like Herr Wertheimer had every opportunity to be happy and never even once took advantage of this opportunity, she said. Such a noble house and so much unhappiness in one person, she said. Basically Wertheimer's suicide didn't come as a surprise to her, but he shouldn't have done that, hanged himself from a tree in Zizers right in front of his sister's house, she wouldn't forgive him for that one. The way she said *Herr Wertheimer* was moving and sickening at the same time. *Once I went to him to ask for money, but he didn't give me any,* she said, *I could have used some cash for a new refrigerator. But they zip their pockets shut, those rich people,* she said, *as soon as you ask for money.* And yet Wertheimer had thrown millions out the window for the fun of it. She considered me to be like Wertheimer, well-to-do, in fact rich and inhuman, for she said spontaneously that all well-to-do and rich people are inhuman. But was *she* human then? I had asked her, to which she gave no answer. She stood up and went over to the beer-truck drivers

who had parked their huge truck in front of the
inn. I was thinking about what the innkeeper had
said and for that reason didn't get up right away
to go to Traich but remained sitting in order to
observe the beer-truck drivers and especially the
innkeeper, who without a doubt was on more intimate terms with the beer-truck drivers than with
any of her other customers. Beer-truck drivers
have fascinated me since my earliest childhood, so
too that day. I was fascinated by the way they
unloaded the beer kegs and rolled them through
the lobby, then tapped the first one for the innkeeper and sat down with her at the next table.
As a child I had wanted to become a beer-truck
driver, admired beer-truck drivers, I thought,
couldn't look often enough at beer-truck drivers.
Sitting at the next table and watching the beer-
truck drivers I again fell prey to this sentiment
from my childhood, but I didn't dwell on it for
long, instead I got up and left the Dichtel Mill for
Traich, not without having told the innkeeper that
I would be back toward evening or even earlier,
depending, and that I was counting on an evening
meal. While going out I heard the beer-truck drivers ask the innkeeper who I was and since I have
sharper ears than anybody I also heard her whisper
my name and add that I was a friend of Wertheimer's, the fool who'd killed himself in Switzerland. Basically I would have preferred to sit in
the restaurant and listen to the beer-truck drivers
and the innkeeper instead of going to Traich now,
I thought while leaving, would have liked most of

all to sit at the same table with the beer-truck drivers and drink a glass of beer with them. Again and again we picture ourselves sitting together with the people we feel drawn to all our lives, precisely these so-called simple people, whom naturally we imagine much differently from the way they truly are, for if we actually sit down with them we see that they aren't the way we've pictured them and that we absolutely don't belong with them, as we've talked ourselves into believing, and we get rejected at their table and in their midst as we logically should get after sitting down at their table and believing we belonged with them or we could sit with them for even the shortest time without being punished, which is the biggest mistake, I thought. All our lives we yearn to be with these people and want to reach out to them and when we realize what we feel for them are rejected by them and indeed in the most brutal fashion. Wertheimer often described how he always failed in his effort to fit in, to be together with so-called simple folk and thus with the so-called people, and he often reported that he went to the Dichtel Mill with the idea of sitting at the table of simple people, only to have to admit after the first such attempt that it was a mistake to think that individuals like him, Wertheimer, or like me could just sit down at the table of simple people. Individuals like us have cut themselves off from the table of simple people at an early age, he said, as I recall, have been born at quite a different table, he said, not at the table of simple people. Individuals like us are naturally drawn to the table of simple people, he said. But we have no business sitting at the table of simple people, as he said, as I recall. To lead a beer-truck driver's existence, I thought, to load and unload beer kegs day after day and roll them through the lobbies of inns throughout Upper Austria and always sit down with these same decrepit innkeepers and fall into bed dead-tired every day for thirty years, for forty years. I took a deep breath and went as fast as I could to Traich. In the country we're confronted with all the unresolvable problems of the world for all time and in a much more drastic manner than in the city, where, if we want to, we can completely anonymize ourselves, I thought, the hideousness and awfulness of the country hit us *right* in the face and we can't get away from them, and this hideousness and awfulness, if we live in the country, are sure to destroy us in the shortest time, that hasn't changed, I thought, since I've been away. If I go back to Desselbrunn I'll definitely go to rack and ruin, a return to Desselbrunn is out of the question, not even after five, six years, I said to myself, and the longer I stay away the more necessary it is for me not to go back to Desselbrunn, to stay in Madrid or in another big city, I said to myself, just not in the country and never again in Upper Austria, I thought. It was cold and windy. The absolute madness of going to Traich, of having got out in Attnang-Puchheim, gone to Wankham, came to my mind. In this region Wertheimer had *had* to go crazy, indeed in the

end lose his mind, I thought, and I said to myself
that he always was exactly *the loser* that Glenn
Gould had always spoken of, Wertheimer was a
typical dead-end guy, I said to myself, he was sure
to go from one dead end to another dead end, for
Traich had always been a dead end, as was later
Vienna, naturally Salzburg too, for Salzburg had
been nothing but an uninterrupted dead end for
him, the Mozarteum nothing but a dead end, just
as the Vienna Academy, just as the whole business
of studying piano had been a dead end, in general
people like him have a choice only between one
dead end and another one, I said to myself, without ever being able to extricate themselves from
this dead-end mechanism. *The loser was a born
loser*, I thought, *he has always been the loser* and
if we observe the people around us carefully we
notice that these people consist almost entirely of
losers like him, I said to myself, of dead-end types
like Wertheimer, whom Glenn Gould had pegged
the moment he saw him as a dead-end type and
loser and whom Glenn Gould had also first called
the *loser* in his ruthless but thoroughly open
Canadian-American manner, Glenn Gould had
said out loud and without any embarrassment
what the others *also* thought but never said out
loud, because this ruthless and open, yet healthy
American-Canadian manner isn't their own, I said
to myself, they all saw the *loser* in Wertheimer,
though of course hadn't dared to call him the *loser*;
but perhaps with their lack of imagination they
never even dreamed of such a nickname, I thought,

which Glenn Gould had coined the moment he
saw Wertheimer, sharp-eyed, as I have to say,
without having observed him for very long he
came up with the *loser* immediately, unlike me,
who came up with the notion of dead-end types
only after observing him and living with him for
years. We always have to deal with losers and
dead-end types like him, I said to myself and lowered my head into the wind. We have the greatest
trouble saving ourselves from these losers and
these dead-end types, for these losers and these
dead-end types risk everything on terrorizing the
people around them, killing off their fellow human
beings, I said to myself. Despite their weakness
and precisely because of their weak constitution
they have the capacity to devastate the people
around them, I thought. They are more ruthless
with the people around them and with their fellow
human beings, I said to myself, than we can initially imagine, and when we discover what makes
them tick, discover this deep-rooted loser mechanism and dead-end-type mechanism, it's usually
too late to escape, they drag you down with all
their might, wherever they can, I said to myself,
for them any victim will do, even their own sister,
I thought. They get the most profit out of their
unhappiness, their loser mechanism, I said to myself on the way to Traich, even though this profit
is naturally of no use to them in the final analysis.
Wertheimer always set about his life with false
assumptions, I said to myself, unlike Glenn who
always set about his existence with the right as-

sumptions. Wertheimer even envied Glenn Gould his death, I said to myself, couldn't even put up with Glenn Gould's death and killed himself a short while thereafter and in truth the crucial factor for his suicide wasn't his sister's departure for Switzerland but the unbearableness of Glenn Gould, as I must say, suffering a fatal stroke at the height of his artistic powers. At first Wertheimer couldn't bear the fact that Glenn Gould played the piano better than he, that he was suddenly the genius Glenn Gould, I thought, world famous to boot, and then finally that he suffered a fatal stroke at the height of his genius and his world fame, I thought. Against all this Wertheimer had only his own death, death by his own hand, I thought. In an excess of megalomania he got into the train for Chur, I said to myself now, and went to Zizers and hanged himself in front of Frau Duttweiler's house, shamelessly. What could I possibly have talked about with the Duttweilers? I asked myself and answered myself immediately with a word I actually said out loud: *nothing*. Should I have told his sister what in truth I thought and still think of Wertheimer, her brother? I thought. It would have been the greatest foolishness, I said to myself. I would have only annoyed the Duttweiler woman with my chatter and it wouldn't have got me further. But I should have refused the Duttweilers' invitation to lunch more politely, I thought now, I actually refused their invitation not only impolitely but in an inadmissible tone of voice, brusquely, offended them, which I couldn't accept now. We behave unjustly, offend people simply to avoid a more difficult moment, an unpleasant confrontation, I thought, for the confrontation with the Duttweilers after Wertheimer's funeral would have certainly been everything but pleasant, I would have again mentioned things that were better left unmentioned, things concerning Wertheimer, and with all the injustice and exaggeration that have become my fate, in a word with the subjectivity I myself have always detested but from which I have never been immune. And the Duttweilers would have pieced together Wertheimerian connections in their own way, which would have produced an equally false and unjust picture of Wertheimer, I said to myself. We constantly portray and judge people only in false terms, we judge them unjustly and portray them meanly, I said to myself, in every instance, no matter how we portray, no matter how we judge them. Such a lunch in Chur with the Duttweilers would have produced nothing but misunderstandings and in the end brought both sides to despair, I thought. So I was right in refusing their invitation and returning to Austria immediately, I thought, even if I shouldn't have gotten out in Attnang-Puchheim, I should have returned to Vienna immediately, gone to my apartment, spent the night and left for Madrid, I thought. The sentimental aspect of interrupting my trip in Attnang-Puchheim for this disgusting but necessary night in the inn at Wankham in order to visit Wertheimer's hunting lodge in Traich was inex-

cusable. At least I could have asked the Duttweilers who was now living in Traich, for on my way
to Traich I didn't have the slightest idea who could
be in Traich now, I couldn't rely on the innkeeper's information, she always talks a lot of nonsense, I thought, like all innkeepers, a lot of beside-
the-point gibberish. And it's even possible that
Frau Duttweiler herself is already in Traich, I
thought, that would be the most natural thing in
the world, that is that she left Chur for Traich
early, unlike my evening departure, perhaps in the
afternoon or even at noon. Who else but his sister
should take over Traich now, I thought, who, now
that Wertheimer is dead and buried in Chur, has
no reason to fear him anymore. Her tormentor is
dead, I thought, her destroyer has reached the end
of his life, is no longer here, will never again have
anything to say about how she leads her life. As
always I was exaggerating now too, and to my
own mind it was disturbing to suddenly hear myself call Wertheimer the tormentor and destroyer
of his sister, I thought, I always behave this way
with others, unjustly, indeed criminally. I have
always suffered from being unjust, I thought. Herr
Duttweiler, who had struck me as so repulsive at
our first meeting and perhaps is not at all that
repulsive, as I now thought, surely has no interest
in Traich, in general hasn't the slightest interest in
Wertheimer interests, I said to myself, it looks as
if what Wertheimer left behind in Traich and Vienna didn't interest him at all, I thought, at most,
Duttweiler is interested in the money Wertheimer

left behind, not at all in the rest of the Wertheimer
property, but the sister must be deeply interested
in it for I can't imagine, I thought, that in marrying
Duttweiler she has separated herself so radically
and definitively from her brother that her brother's
estate would be a matter of complete indifference
to her, quite the contrary, I now suspected that
now of all times, liberated by her brother through
his so to speak demonstrative suicide, she will suddenly take an interest in all Wertheimer matters
with the intensity with which she was previously
not interested in them and that perhaps now she
is even interested in her brother's so-called *human-
science estate*. In my mind, as they say, I pictured
her now in Traich, sitting over thousands, if not
hundreds of thousands, of her brother's notes and
studying them. Then I thought again that Wertheimer hadn't left a single note behind, which
would be more characteristic of him than a so-
called literary estate, which he personally never
held in high regard, as I always heard him say in
any case, even though I can't say he said it seriously, I thought. For very often people who work
with products of the intellect say they don't hold
something in high regard and on the contrary hold
it in very high regard indeed, just won't admit it
because they're ashamed of such inferior work, as
they call it, bad-mouth their work so as not to have
to be publicly ashamed of it at least, Wertheimer
could have been operating with smoke-screen tac-
tics like that when talking about his so-called human sciences, I thought, that would be just like

him. In that case I would actually have the opportunity to look into this intellectual work of his, I thought. It suddenly had got so cold that I had to turn up the collar of my coat. Again and again we look for the cause of something and little by little go from one possibility to the other, I thought, that Glenn's death is the actual cause for Wertheimer's death, I thought again and again, not that Wertheimer's sister moved to Zizers to be with Duttweiler. The cause, and we not only say this, always lies much deeper and it lies in the Goldberg Variations that Glenn played in Salzburg during Horowitz's course, *the Well-Tempered Clavier is the cause*, I thought, it doesn't lie in the fact that Wertheimer's sister cut herself off from her brother at the age of forty-six. Wertheimer's sister is actually innocent in Wertheimer's death, I thought, Wertheimer wanted, I thought, to shift the blame for his suicide to his sister, to deflect attention from the fact that nothing but Glenn's interpretation of the *Goldberg Variations* as well as his *Well-Tempered Clavier* was to blame for his suicide, as indeed for his disastrous life. But Wertheimer's disaster had already started the moment Glenn called Wertheimer *the loser*, what Wertheimer had always known Glenn said out loud, abruptly and without bias, as I have to say, in his Canadian-American way, Glenn mortally wounded Wertheimer *with his loser*, I thought, not because Wertheimer heard this concept for the first time but because Wertheimer, without *knowing this word loser*, had long been familiar *with the concept of loser,* but Glenn Gould *said the word loser out loud in a crucial moment,* I thought. We say a word and destroy a person, although the person we've destroyed, at the moment we say out loud the word that destroys him, doesn't take notice of this deadly fact, I thought. A person confronted with such a deadly word and deadly concept still has no idea of the deadly effect of this word and its concept, I thought. Even before Horowitz's course had begun Glenn said the word *loser* to Wertheimer, I thought, I could even specify the precise hour in which Glenn said the word *loser* to Wertheimer. We say a deadly word to a person and at that moment are naturally unaware that we have actually said a deadly word to him, I thought. Twenty-eight years after Glenn said to Wertheimer at the Mozarteum that he was a *loser* and twelve years after he said it to him in America, Wertheimer killed himself. Suicides are ridiculous, Wertheimer often said, the ones who hang themselves are the most disgusting, he also said, I thought, now of course it's striking that he often spoke about suicide, and in doing so always more or less made fun of suicide victims, as I have to say, always talked about suicide and suicide victims as if neither one nor the other had anything to do with him, as if one like the other was out of the question for him. *I* was a suicide type, he often said, I recalled on the way to Traich, *I* was the one in danger, not he. And he had also thought his sister capable of suicide, probably because he best knew her actual situation, was familiar with the absolute hopelessness of her situation, like no other, because he, as he often said, thought he could see through his creation. But his sister, instead of killing herself, fled to Duttweiler in Switzerland, got herself married to Herr Duttweiler, I thought. Wertheimer finally killed himself in a way he always termed repulsive and disgusting, and of all places in Switzerland, his sister went to Switzerland to marry this wealthy chemical Duttweiler instead of killing herself, he went there however to hang himself from a tree in Zizers, I thought. He wanted to study with Horowitz, I thought, and was destroyed by Glenn Gould. Glenn died at the *ideal moment*, Wertheimer however didn't kill himself at the ideal moment, I thought. If I really have another go at my description of Glenn Gould, I thought, I will have to incorporate *his* description of Wertheimer in it and it's questionable who will be the focus of this account, Glenn Gould or Wertheimer, I thought. I'll start with Glenn Gould, with the *Goldberg Variations* and with the *Well-Tempered Clavier*, but Wertheimer will play a crucial role in this account as far as I'm concerned, since from my point of view Glenn Gould was always linked to Wertheimer, no matter in what respect, and vice versa Wertheimer with Glenn Gould and perhaps all in all Glenn Gould does play a greater role in Wertheimer's life than the other way around. The actual starting point has to be Horowitz's course, I thought, the sculptor's house in Leopoldskron, the fact that we came together completely by chance twenty-eight years ago was crucial for our lives, I thought. Wertheimer's Bösendorfer against Glenn Gould's Steinway, I thought, *Glenn Gould's Goldberg Variations against Wertheimer's Art of the Fugue*, I thought. Glenn Gould surely doesn't owe Horowitz his genius, I thought, but Wertheimer is perfectly entitled to blame *Horowitz* for his downfall and destruction, I thought, for Wertheimer, attracted by the name Horowitz, had gone to Salzburg, without the name Horowitz he would never have gone to Salzburg, at least not in that fateful year. Whereas the *Goldberg Variations* were composed for the sole purpose of helping an insomniac put up with the insomnia he had suffered from all his life, I thought, they killed Wertheimer. They were originally composed *to delight the soul* and almost two hundred and fifty years later they have killed a hopeless person, i.e., Wertheimer, I thought on my way to Traich. If Wertheimer hadn't walked past room thirty-three on the second floor of the Mozarteum twenty-eight years ago, precisely at four in the afternoon, he wouldn't have hanged himself twenty-eight years later in Zizers bei Chur, I thought. Wertheimer's fate was to have walked past room thirty-three in the Mozarteum at the precise moment when Glenn Gould was playing the so-called *aria* in that room. Regarding this event Wertheimer reported to me that he stopped at the door of room thirty-three, listening to Glenn play until the end of the *aria*. Then I understood what shock is, I thought now. The so-called wunderkind Glenn

Gould had meant nothing to us, Wertheimer and me, and we wouldn't have given it a second thought if we had known something about him, I thought. Glenn Gould was no wunderkind, from the very beginning he was a keyboard genius, I thought, even as a child simple mastery wasn't enough for him. We, Wertheimer and myself, had our so-called isolation houses in the country and were running away from them. Glenn Gould built himself an isolation cage, as he called his studio, in America, close to New York. If *he* named Wertheimer *the loser*, I want to call him, Glenn, the *refuser*, I thought. I have to call the year 1953 the *fateful* one for Wertheimer, for in 1953 Glenn Gould played the *Goldberg Variations* in our sculptor's house for no one else but Wertheimer and me, years before he became world famous overnight, as they say, with these same *Goldberg Variations*. In 1953 Glenn Gould destroyed Wertheimer, I thought. In 1954 we hadn't had any news from him, in 1955 he played the *Goldberg Variations* in the Festspielhaus, Wertheimer and I listened to him from the catwalk together with a group of stagehands who otherwise had never heard a piano concert but were crazy about Glenn's playing. Glenn, who always *broke into a sweat*, Glenn, the Canadian-American who without embarrassment called Wertheimer the *loser*, Glenn, who laughed in the *Ganshof* the way I never before and never again heard anyone laugh, I thought, comparing him to Wertheimer, who was the exact opposite of Glenn Gould, even though I can't describe this opposite, but I'll make an attempt, I thought, when I start again my *Essay on Glenn*. I'll lock myself in my apartment in the Calle del Prado and write about Glenn and all by itself the Wertheimer problem will become clear to me, I thought. By writing about Glenn Gould I'll put my thoughts about Wertheimer in order, I thought on my way to Traich. I was walking much too fast and during my walk had trouble breathing, the old lung illness which has plagued me now for over two decades. By writing about the one (Glenn Gould), I will order my thoughts about the other (Wertheimer), I thought, by listening again and again to the *Goldberg Variations* (and the *Art of the Fugue*) of the one (Glenn), in order to write about them, I will know more and more about the art (or the nonart!) of the other (Wertheimer) and be able to write it down, I thought, and all at once I longed to be in Madrid and my Calle del Prado, in my Spanish home, as I had never longed to be anywhere else before. Basically my walk to Traich was depressing and, as I thought again and again, will prove futile. Or won't be *completely futile*, as I thought at the moment, I thought, and went faster toward Traich. I knew the hunting lodge, my first impression was that nothing had changed, my second that it had to be an ideal structure for a person like Wertheimer but then never was the ideal structure for him, quite the contrary. As my Desselbrunn also never was and still isn't the ideal structure for me, but the opposite, as I thought, even if everything gave the impression that Desselbrunn was ideal for me (and people like me). We see a structure and believe it is ideal for us (and for people like us) and it's absolutely not ideal for our purposes and for the purposes of people like us, I thought. Just as we see a person as the ideal one for us, whereas he is everything but ideal for us, I thought. My assumption that Traich was locked up turned out to be false, the garden gate was open, even the front door was open as I saw from afar and I went right through the garden and in the front door. The woodsman Franz (Kohlroser), whom I knew, greeted me. He had just heard about Wertheimer's suicide that morning, everybody was horrified, he said. Wertheimer's sister had announced she would be coming in the next few days, he said, the Duttweiler woman. I should come inside, in the meantime he had opened all the windows to air out the house, he said, unfortunately his co-worker had gone to Linz for three days, he was alone in Traich, *a stroke of luck that you came*, he said. Whether I wanted a drink of water, he asked, he recalled immediately that I'm a water drinker. No, I said, not now, I'd had tea at the inn in Wankham where I planned to spend the night. As always Wertheimer had gone away for two or three days, of course he had *said* that he was going to Chur to visit his sister, said Franz. He hadn't noticed anything striking or odd about Wertheimer when the latter left Traich in the chauffeured car, Franz said, he took to Attnang-Puchheim, the car was certainly still parked in the lot in front of the

station. Franz calculated that twelve days had
passed since his master had left for Switzerland
and that, as he first learned from me, the latter
had already been dead for eleven days. *Hanged*, I
said to Franz. He, Franz, feared that now, after
the death of Wertheimer, of his provider, everything in Traich might change, especially since this
Frau Duttweiler was a *strange person*, he hadn't
said that he now feared the appearance of Frau
Duttweiler, but he did suggest he was frightened
that, under the influence of her Swiss husband, she
would completely change things in Traich, maybe
she'll sell Traich, Franz said, for what should she
do with Traich now that she's married herself off
to Switzerland, and to such a wealthy part of Switzerland. For Traich had been completely her
brother's house, had been added on to and re-
modeled and equipped completely for his needs
and in such a way that it actually was contrary to
everybody else's nature, as I thought, in a truly
Wertheimerian way it was only for him. Wertheimer's sister never felt comfortable in Traich
and her brother, as Franz said, had never let her
develop in Traich, he'd never granted any of her
wishes concerning Traich, he, Wertheimer, always
quashed her plans to adapt Traich to her taste,
incidentally he always *tormented the poor woman*,
as Franz expressed himself. The Duttweiler
woman must almost hate Traich, he claimed, for
she hadn't spent a single happy day in Traich,
Franz said. He recalled that once, without asking
him whether her brother would mind, she'd

opened the curtains in his room, at which point
he drove her out of his room, furious. If she
wanted to invite guests he wouldn't allow it, said
Franz, she also wasn't permitted to dress the way
she wanted, had always had to wear the clothes
that *he* wanted to see on her, even during the cold-
est weather she was never allowed to put on her
Tyrolian hat, for her brother hated Tyrolian hats
and hated, as I also know, everything connected
with Tyrolian folk costume, as of course he himself
never wore anything that even vaguely recalled
Tyrolian folk costume, thus here, in this region,
he naturally always stood out, for here everybody
always wears Tyrolian folk costume, above all
clothes that are made from coarse loden wool,
which is actually ideally suited for the quite dreadful climatic conditions in the lower Alps, I
thought, he found Tyrolian folk costume, like
anything that even reminded him of Tyrolian folk
costume, deeply repugnant. When his sister once
asked him for permission to go to the so-called
Bäckerberg to a May Day dance with a woman
from the neighborhood, he wouldn't allow it, said
Franz. And of course they had to do without the
priest's company, for Wertheimer hated Catholicism, which his sister, as I also know, had completely fallen prey to in the last years. One of his
habits had been to ask his sister, in the middle of
the night, to come to his room to play something
by Handel on the old harmonium he had standing
in his room, Franz actually said *Handel*. The sister
had had to get up at one or two in the morning

and put on her dressing gown and go to his room
and sit down at the harmonium in the unheated
room and play Handel, Franz said, which naturally resulted, he said, in her getting a cold and
constantly suffering from colds in Traich. He,
Wertheimer, hadn't taken good care of his sister,
Franz said. He would have her play Handel for
an hour on the old harmonium, said Franz, and
then the next morning at breakfast, which they
took together in the kitchen, he would tell her that
her harmonium playing had been unbearable. He
would have her play him something in order to
fall back to sleep, said Franz, for Herr Wertheimer
always suffered from his *insomnia,* and then would
tell her the next morning that she had played *like
a pig.* Wertheimer had always had to force his
sister to come to Traich, he, Franz, even believed
that Wertheimer had hated his sister but hadn't
been able to get along in Traich without her, and
I thought that Wertheimer always spoke of solitude without ever actually being able to be alone,
he was no *solitude type,* I thought, and so on his
visits to Traich he always took along his sister,
whom he loved by the way, although he hated
her like no one else in the world, in order to *misuse* her in his way. When it got cold, as Franz
said, he would have his sister heat his room,
whereas she wasn't allowed to heat her room. She
always had to take her walks in the direction prescribed by her brother and also only for the duration prescribed by her brother and had to
observe precisely the time he had determined for

her walks, as Franz said. Mostly she would sit in her room, as Franz said, but she wasn't allowed to listen to music, her brother couldn't stand her listening to a record, which she would have liked to do. He, Franz, still distinctly recalled the two Wertheimers' childhood when the two would arrive eagerly in Traich, fun-loving children who were ready for anything, as Franz said. The hunting lodge had been the favorite playground of the two Wertheimer children. When the Wertheimer family was in England, during the Nazi period, as Franz said, when a Nazi administrator had lodged in Traich, it had been frightfully quiet in Traich, everything went to seed in that period, nothing was repaired, everything left to itself, for the administrator hadn't taken care of anything, a decrepit Nazi count had lived in Traich but didn't understand a thing, as Franz said, the Nazi count *almost ruined* Traich. After the Wertheimers came back from England, at first to Vienna, only much later to Traich, as Franz said, they had kept to themselves, hadn't wanted any contact with their neighbors. He, Franz, had come back into their service, they had always paid him well and *always credited him* for having remained faithful to them even during Nazi rule and during their entire England period, as he put it. The fact that he took better care of Traich in the so-called Nazi period than the Nazis would have liked, as Franz put it, not only got him a warning from the Nazi authorities, it also landed him in jail in Wels for two months, since then he hated Wels, wouldn't go there anymore, even for the local carnival. *Herr Wertheimer hadn't wanted to let his sister go to church*, said Franz, but she went *to evening mass in secret*. The parents of the young Wertheimers hadn't gotten much enjoyment out of Traich anymore, said Franz, with whom I was standing in the kitchen, they died in an accident much too early. They were on their way to Merano, said Franz. Herr Wertheimer senior didn't want to go to Merano, but *she* wanted to, he said. They only found the car two weeks after it had fallen over a cliff in Bressanone, he said. The Wertheimers had relatives in Merano, I thought. Wertheimer's great-grandfather had hired him, Franz, in Traich. Even his father had spent his life working for the Wertheimers. Their employers had always been good to all of them, hadn't let any debts pile up, and so in return they quite naturally never had any complaints, as Franz put it. He couldn't imagine what would happen now with Traich. What I thought of Herr Duttweiler, Franz wanted to know, to which I only shook my head. Perhaps, as Franz put it, Wertheimer's sister will come to Traich to sell Traich. I don't think so, I said, I absolutely couldn't imagine that the Duttweiler woman would sell Traich, although I thought it perfectly possible that she was thinking of selling Traich, but I didn't tell Franz what I was thinking, I said very clearly, no, I don't think the Duttweiler woman will sell Traich, I really don't think so. I wanted to calm Franz, who was naturally worried about losing his lifelong employment. It's of course quite possible that the Duttweiler woman, Wertheimer's sister, will come to Traich and sell Traich, perhaps as soon as possible, I thought, but I said to Franz I was convinced that Wertheimer's sister, *the sister of my friend*, I expressly emphasized, wouldn't sell Traich, they have so much money, the Duttweilers, I said to Franz, that they don't need to sell Traich, while I was thinking that precisely because the Duttweilers have so much money they're perhaps thinking of simply getting rid of Traich as soon as possible, they certainly won't sell Traich, I said, and was thinking, they may well sell Traich immediately, and I said to Franz, he could be certain that here in Traich nothing would change, while I was thinking that perhaps everything will change in Traich. The Duttweiler woman will come here and take care of everything that has to be taken care of, I said to Franz, will take the estate in hand, I said, and I asked Franz whether Frau Duttweiler was coming to Traich alone or with her husband. He didn't know, she hadn't told him that. I drank a glass of water and thought while I was drinking that in Traich I have always drunk the best water of my life. Before Wertheimer went to Switzerland, he invited a crowd of people to Traich for two weeks, it took days for him, Franz, and his co-worker to get everything back in shape, they came from Vienna, said Franz, had never been in Traich before but were quite obviously good friends of his master. I've already heard about these people from the innkeeper, I said, that these people traipsed through town, artists, I said, probably musicians, and I wondered whether these people weren't artists and musicians with whom Wertheimer once went to school, conservatory colleagues as it were from his time at the conservatories in Salzburg and Vienna. In the end we remember all the students we've gone to school with and invite them to our homes only to find out that we no longer have the least thing in common with them, I thought. Wertheimer also invited me to his house, I thought at that moment, and with what relentlessness; I thought of his letters and above all the last card he sent to me in Madrid, naturally I now had a guilty conscience, for I realized I was connected with these *artist invitations* on his part, but he hadn't mentioned these people, I thought, and I would never have come to Traich to see all these people, I said to myself. What Wertheimer must have gone through that he, who never invited anyone to Traich, suddenly invited dozens of people to Traich, even if they were former conservatory colleagues, whom otherwise he always detested; there was always at least a hint of scorn in his voice when he spoke of his former conservatory colleagues, I thought. What the innkeeper only alluded to and what she of course couldn't know more about than that they traipsed through town, laughing and finally kicking up a row in their gaudy artist costumes, in their gaudy artist parade, suddenly became clear to me: Wertheimer invited his former conservatory colleagues to Traich and didn't chase them away immediately but let them

run wild *against himself* for days, even weeks. A
fact that had to strike me as totally incomprehen-
sible, since for decades Wertheimer didn't want to
have anything to do with these conservatory colleagues, never wanted to hear anything about them
and even in his sleep he wouldn't have had the idea
of inviting them one fine day to Traich, which
apparently he now had done, and between this
absurd invitation and his suicide there must be a
relationship, I thought. Those people ruined a lot
of things in Traich, said Franz. Wertheimer had
been *exuberant* with them, which by the way
Franz had also noticed, he became a totally different person in their company during those days
and weeks. Franz also said that the people had
spent more than two weeks in Traich and let
Wertheimer provide for them, he actually said *provide*, just as the innkeeper had said in relation to
these people from Vienna. After this whole crowd,
which hadn't kept quiet a single night, got roaring
drunk every night, finally went away, Wertheimer
got into bed and didn't get up for two days and
nights, said Franz, who in the meantime had
cleaned up the dirt from these city people, in general brought the entire house back into a *decent
human condition*, in order to spare Herr Wertheimer the sight of Traich's devastation when he
got up, said Franz. What he, Franz, particularly
noticed, that is that Wertheimer had had a piano
delivered from Salzburg in order to play it, certainly should have some meaning for me. A day
before the people from Vienna arrived he had *or-*

dered a piano for himself in Salzburg and had had it brought to Traich and played it, at first only for himself, then, when the whole company was assembled, for this company, Wertheimer played Bach for them, Franz said, Handel and Bach, which he hadn't done for more than ten years. Wertheimer, said Franz, played Bach on the piano without stopping until finally the company couldn't take it anymore and left the house. The company was barely back in the house before he would start playing Bach again until they went out. Perhaps he wanted to drive them all crazy with his piano playing, said Franz, for no sooner had they stepped inside than he would start playing Bach and Handel for them, playing until they ran away, outside, and when they came back they had to put up with his piano playing again. It went on this way for over two weeks, said Franz, who soon had to think his master had lost his mind. He thought that the guests wouldn't put up with it for long, that Wertheimer always played the piano for them without stopping, but even so they had stayed two weeks, *more than two weeks*, without exception, he, Franz, suspected, since he saw that Wertheimer actually drove his guests crazy with his piano playing, that Wertheimer bribed his guests, gave them money so they would stay in Traich, for without such a bribe, that is without *money in return*, said Franz, they surely never would have stayed more than two weeks to let themselves be driven crazy by Wertheimer's piano playing, and I thought that Franz was probably correct in assuming that Wertheimer had given these people money, actually bribed them, even though perhaps not with money but with something else, so that they stayed two weeks, indeed *more* than two weeks. For he surely wanted them to stay more than two weeks, I thought, otherwise they wouldn't have stayed more than two weeks, I know Wertheimer too well not to think him capable of that kind of blackmail. Always only Bach and Handel, said Franz, without stopping, *until he blacked out*. Finally Wertheimer had a *king's meal*, as Franz put it, brought up to the large dining room for all these people and told them that they all had to be gone the next morning, he, Franz, had heard with his own ears how Wertheimer said he no longer wanted to see their faces the next morning. He actually had taxis from Attnang-Puchheim ordered for every one of them for the next morning and indeed for four o'clock in the morning and they all drove off in these taxis, leaving the house in a catastrophic state. He, Franz, began cleaning up the mess immediately and without delay, he couldn't have known, as he said, that his employer would stay in bed for two days and two nights, but that had been a good thing, for Wertheimer had needed the rest and he undoubtedly would have had a stroke, so Franz, if he'd seen what a state those people had left his house in, they shamelessly *destroyed* some of the furniture, said Franz, overturned chairs and even tables before leaving Traich and shattered a few mirrors and a few glass doors, probably out of arrogance, said Franz, out of anger at having been exploited by Wertheimer, I thought. A piano actually stood where no piano had stood for a decade, now there's a piano, as I saw after going up to the second floor with Franz. I was interested in Wertheimer's notes, I had said to Franz while still downstairs in the kitchen, without hesitating Franz then led me up to the second floor. The piano was *an Ehrbar* and worth nothing. And it was, as I noticed right away, totally out of tune, an amateur's instrument through and through, I thought. I wasn't able to keep myself from sitting down at the piano but then I shut the cover immediately. I was interested in the notes, the slips of paper Wertheimer had written, I said to Franz, whether he could tell me where these notes were. He didn't know what notes I meant, said Franz, only then reporting the fact that Wertheimer, on the day he had ordered a piano for himself *at the Mozarteum,* that is one day before that crowd of people came to Traich who more or less devastated Traich, had burned entire stacks of paper in the so-called downstairs stove, that is the stove in the dining room. He, Franz, had helped his master with this task, for the stacks of notes were so large and heavy that Wertheimer hadn't been able to drag them downstairs alone. He had taken out hundreds and thousands of notes from all his drawers and closets and with his, Franz's, help had dragged them down to the dining room to burn the notes, solely for the purpose of burning the notes he'd had Franz light the dining room stove at five in the morning that day, said Franz. When the notes were all burned, *all that writing*, as Franz expressed himself, he, Wertheimer, called up Salzburg and ordered the piano and Franz distinctly recalled that during this telephone call his master kept insisting that they send *a completely worthless, a horribly untuned grand piano* to Traich. *A completely worthless instrument, a horribly untuned instrument*, Wertheimer is supposed to have repeated over and over on the phone, said Franz. A few hours later four people delivered the piano to Traich and put it in the former music room, said Franz, and Wertheimer gave the men who had put the piano in the music room *a huge tip*, if he wasn't mistaken, and he wasn't mistaken, he said, *two thousand schillings*. The deliverymen weren't out the door, said Franz, before Wertheimer sat down at the piano and began playing. It was awful, said Franz. He, Franz, had thought his master had lost his mind. But he, Franz, hadn't wanted to believe in Wertheimer's insanity and hadn't taken the nonetheless curious behavior of Wertheimer, his master, seriously. If I had any interest in the matter, Franz said to me, he would describe to me the days and weeks that then took place in Traich. I asked Franz to leave me alone in Wertheimer's room for a while and put on Glenn's *Goldberg Variations*, which I had seen lying on Wertheimer's record player, which was still open.

AFTERWORD

One might just be happy a few times a year
in this city, walking across the Kohlmarkt
or the Graben, strolling down
the Singerstrasse in the spring air
　　　　　Thomas Bernhard, Heldenplatz

During his lifetime Thomas Bernhard's texts provoked more than the ordinary share of scandals.
But perhaps the most enduring scandal will turn
out to be his very last text, his will: "Whatever I
have written, whether published by me during my
lifetime or as part of my literary papers still existing
after my death, shall not be performed, printed or
even recited for the duration of legal copyright
within the borders of Austria, however this state
identifies itself." Bernhard had taken care not to
reveal the contents of this will before he died; in
fact, he even stipulated that news of his death not
be announced until he was buried. This parting
slap in the face of his native country thus came
not only as a surprise; it came from the hand of a
dead man, whose laughter rang out from the grave.

To be sure, it was absurd laughter that had

something of a bad and willfully unpatriotic joke. But then so did most of Bernhard's literary works. In his last play, *Heldenplatz*, one of the members of a Jewish family that has recently returned to Vienna characterizes the country as a pigsty with only "black" (i.e., fascist) and "red" (socialist) pigs living there:

> *In this most horrendous of states*
> *you have only a choice*
> *between black pigs and red pigs*
> *an unbearable stench from the Royal Palace*
> *and Ballhaus Square and Parliament*
> *spreads over this completely disgusting and*
>   *decrepit country*
> (shouts)
> *This tiny state is a gigantic dunghill*

"The whole thing was an absurd idea / to come back to Vienna," the same character concludes in the very last lines of the play. "But of course the world consists only of absurd ideas."

Not to hear the laughter behind these last texts of Bernhard's would be a mistake, for it would mean reading him literally, hence missing the dimension of irony, exaggeration, and pose that characterized all his writings and public statements to the very last. That Bernhard maintained this dimension even where it supposedly doesn't belong, that quite literal and serious legal battles are being fought over the interpretation of his will, only points to his characteristic unwillingness to compromise what he saw as his fundamental task and pleasure as a writer: to denounce, scandalize, and just plain get on people's nerves. "To shake people up, that's my real pleasure," he once admitted. This Bernhard undoubtedly managed to do for most of his life, and to judge from the court battles over his literary estate, he may well be doing it for some time to come.

Not that a serious dose of unassuaged anger wasn't part of Bernhard's vitriolic gestures. But by the same logic that made him refuse the world's distinction between fact and fiction, between legal seriousness and poetic license, so Bernhard always maintained that this animosity was in fact an expression of his deep and abiding love for Austria. He once told a journalist, lowering his eyes and laughing quietly to himself, that he had signed the guestbook in a friend's house as *"die Güte selbst"*—goodness in person. "Everybody was very surprised." But Bernhard meant it, just as he meant it when he claimed that his anti-Austrian, lugubrious, death-obsessed narratives ("automatically black" in George Steiner's phrase) sprang from his sense of humor, of the absurd, even from his "positive" view of life. Hence his refusal to paint utopian or idealistic portraits: "An idealistic literary work can produce disgust in the reader. Whoever sees through the author's intention and recognizes that in reality things are completely different will fall back into negativity." Bernhard's

"negative" books, which make no attempt to pret-
tify or soften reality, should produce the opposite
reaction—cathartic or "tragic" laughter.

Bernhard loved as well as hated his native country, was tied to it by the chains of a passionate
ambivalence, which is the true wellspring of all his
work. Once a court reporter for the left-wing paper *Demokratisches Volksblatt*, Bernhard remained a *"Zeitungsfresser"* all his life, a person
who "devoured" newspapers, local as well as national, gleaning from them his daily ration of outrage, humor, and absurdity. I remember sitting
next to him in his favorite café in Vienna, the Bräu-
nerhof, listening to a steady stream of polemical
and witty commentary on each little story or fact,
watching him return again and again to the newspaper table in search of more reading material. A
master at provoking scandals, he relished reading
about himself. But he also enjoyed the news about
everyday life in small rural towns —land disputes,
court trials, stories of adultery, murder, or suicide—which gave him the ideas for much of his
work. And for this reason it is doubtful whether
he could ever have lived and worked abroad.
Most of Austria's major postwar writers—Canetti,
Celan, Bachmann, Handke—have preferred self-
imposed exile to residence in their native country.
Bernhard, ostensibly the most anti-Austrian of
them all, is one of the few who never left.

But whereas Bernhard both loved and hated
Austria, most Austrians simply hated Bernhard
and would readily have done without his muck-

raking attacks. The scandal provoked by *Heldenplatz* in the fall of 1988 is a case in point. Shortly before the opening, in November, newspapers leaked a few quotes from the play, which, like the above passage, were not exactly measured political assessments of Austria and its inhabitants. Without knowing anything about the play, in what context these passages appeared, or what irony Bernhard might have given them, journalists and politicians felt called upon to protest the use of taxpayers' money for staging such an unpatriotic work in the Burgtheater, Austria's national theater. Kurt Waldheim characterized the play as "an insult to the nation." Popular outrage took to the streets. Normally well-behaved citizens scrawled obscene messages in public places against the ungrateful author, and one elderly lady attacked Bernhard with her umbrella as he was getting on the bus.

Of course there was a deeper reason for Austrians to be upset, as they would learn when the play finally opened. *Heldenplatz* (Heroes' Square) had been commissioned and written that year to "commemorate" the fifty-year anniversary of Austria's *Anschluss* with Nazi Germany. The play begins with the suicide of an eminent Jewish professor who fled Austria in 1938 and lived in exile in England before returning to present-day Vienna. Despairing of the still virulent anti-Semitism he encounters there, he throws himself from the window of his apartment overlooking Heroes' Square, which not coincidentally is the square where thousands of cheering Austrians greeted

Hitler in 1938 and which, also not coincidentally, is adjacent to the offices of Austria's major politicians and the very Burgtheater where the play is performed. Bernhard's sense of dramatic irony and historical context is superbly evident in the play, especially in the final scene, when the professor's aged mother hears recorded chants of "Sieg Heil!" that emerge from the wings (and as if from outside the theater). She is hallucinating, since no one else on stage pays any attention to the chants. But the audience hears them, and as we look about we realize that some of the elderly, elegant spectators must have been on Heroes' Square in 1938 shouting those very words. The voice Bernhard confronts his audience with is its own, the recorded voice of Austria's buried political unconscious.

I tell these stories because most English-speaking readers will not be aware of the political dimension of Bernhard's writing and its reception in Austria. But I also tell them because the scandals in Bernhard's life were inseparable from his work, inseparable because both life and work were meant as a form of satire that would pass judgment on Austria even while laughing at its most egregious examples of political waywardness, provincialism, and human cruelty. In this respect Bernhard continues a long tradition of Austrian satire, from Johann Nestroy to Karl Kraus, Robert Musil, and the experimental poet Ernst Jandl. For *The Loser* is first of all a satire of Austria. It is no accident that the narrator should meet Glenn Gould at the "Judge's Peak" on Monk's Mountain overlooking

Salzburg. Nor that the three protagonists should rent a house that once belonged to a Nazi sculptor whose marble monstrosities still decorate the premises. Remnants of Austria's past live on, and Bernhard was the self-appointed judge who would pass sentence.

Thomas Bernhard was born on 10 February 1931 in a cloister in Heerlen, a small town in Holland near the German and Belgian borders, where his unmarried mother had fled to avoid the scandal that an illegitimate birth would have caused in the Austrian provinces. His father, a peasant whom he never knew except through his mother's bitter reminiscences, died sometime during the war, probably as a Nazi soldier. As a child, he lived with his mother's parents in Vienna and the village of Seekirchen, in impoverished circumstances. By his own account these years were lonely ones, and he felt misunderstood and excluded even within his family. The one exception was his mother's father, the poet and philosopher Johannes Freumbichler, who loved this awkward, strong-willed child and became his mentor. Bernhard later noted that it was his grandfather who instilled in him a fierce intellectual independence, warning him, for instance, not to take school seriously or to believe his teachers.

In 1943 Bernhard was sent to a boarding school in Salzburg, the provincial city that, with Vienna, would eventually form one of the two poles of his love-hate relationship to Austria. He attended the Johanneum Gymnasium briefly, took music lessons, and was considering a career as an opera singer. But his disgust with the school's Catholic piety (which he claimed had merely supplanted the National Socialist piety he witnessed there during the war) led him to abandon his studies and apprentice himself to a grocer outside Salzburg. Lugging heavy sacks of potatoes in a damp cellar brought on a lung illness that almost killed him (at one point he received last rites) and kept him in and out of hospitals for several years. It is in this period, as a kind of therapy, that he began writing: "With death staring me in the face at the sanatorium in Grafenhof I first began to write. And that's perhaps how I cured myself." In 1951 he moved to Vienna to study at the Musik-Akademie, returning to Salzburg the following year, where he enrolled at the Mozarteum and studied music and theater arts; he graduated in 1956 with a thesis on Artaud and Brecht. Apart from several lengthy visits to Poland and a year in London working for the Austrian Cultural Institute, and extended vacations in Mediterranean countries, he lived in Austria on his earnings as a writer, alternating between a small apartment in Vienna and a farmhouse in Ohlsdorf (Upper Austria), not far from Salzburg. He died alone in this farmhouse on 12 February 1989, two days after his fifty-eighth birthday.

Bernhard's first literary attempts in the 1950s and early 1960s were in lyric poetry, the same genre his grandfather had practiced. Morbid, almost hallucinatory verse modeled after Rilke and Trakl, it lacked the humor and dramatic brilliance of his later work and met with scant critical success; Bernhard himself later rejected it. His literary breakthrough came with the novel *Frost* (1963), in which his characteristic prose style—a relentless inner monologue unbroken by any paragraph markings, objective description, or external narrative events—is already fully developed. Bernhard never wavered from this monologistic form and even extended it into the theater, using it in the course of the next twenty-six years for an oeuvre that, although not without its weak moments, has few contemporary equals in quality or size: more than twenty novels or collections of stories, an equal number of plays, a five-volume autobiography, and two full-length scripts for movies based on his stories. For this work Bernhard received all the major Austrian and German awards, although he characteristically used these occasions to lash out at Austrian "philistinism" and "art hatred." His acceptance speech for the Austrian State Prize for Literature in 1967 proved so offensive that it drove the Minister of Culture and a good part of the audience from the room.

The Loser was published in Germany in 1983 and comes at the end of a seven-year period in which Bernhard wrote the five volumes of his autobiography. This sustained examination of the self proved crucial. Whereas the earlier prose works had focused on private stories of madness and human isolation—an unknown painter who destroys his work, a country doctor treating incurably ill patients, an insane count lying alone in his villa—those written after the autobiography project these same scenarios onto the public biographies of people like Wittgenstein, Mendelssohn, or, as in the present case, Glenn Gould. But in each case the public figure serves as a foil for Bernhard himself. Indeed, the novels written after this point—*Wittgenstein's Nephew*, *Woodcutters*, *Old Masters*, and *The Loser*—all walk a very thin line between fact and fiction, borrowing so heavily from the details of Bernhard's real life that he was more than once sued for libel. These later texts are all part of what might be termed Bernhard's imaginary autobiography—his own life story rewritten according to the lives of his artistic and philosophical doubles.

Thus Glenn Gould appears in *The Loser*, at once beguilingly familiar—the "real Glenn Gould," who gave up public concerts at an early age to concentrate on his recordings—and an artificial literary construct that resembles Bernhard and all his fictional alter egos. There is no evidence that Bernhard ever met Gould, and the two certainly didn't study together in Salzburg with Horowitz, as the novel claims. Yet there is a detail in Gould's biography that may well have tickled Bernhard's imagination into using him as a fictional *doppelgänger*. During a European tour in 1958, Gould gave a concert in Salzburg, which Bernhard, given his own music studies there, may well have attended. In any case, years later Gould recalled in one of his self-interviews that the drafty Festspielhaus had brought on a bout of tracheitis that forced him to cancel all concerts, withdraw for a month in the Alps, and lead "the most idyllic and isolated existence." Gould the journalist speaks to Gould the musician thus:

> Since you're obviously a man addicted to symbols . . . it would seem to me that the Festspielhaus—the Felsenreitschule—with its Kafka-like setting at the base of a cliff, with the memory of equestrian mobility haunting its past, and located, moreover, in the birthplace of a composer whose works you have frequently criticized . . . is a place to which a man like yourself, a man in search of martyrdom, should return.

Here perhaps is the original kernel for Bernhard's novel: the "Kafka-like setting" of the Festspielhaus, Gould's respiratory illness and ascetic isolation in the Alps, a "return" to Salzburg, where Bernhard had also studied music so many years ago. . . .

True to his habit, however, Bernhard traffics freely with the details of Gould's biography. The very first page of the novel puts his death at age fifty-one rather than the actual fifty. The Canadian pianist is given a lung disease that he never suffered from; in the novel it becomes his "second art." Gould is said to have cut off relations with his family and withdrawn to a house in the woods near New York. In reality, after giving up concert life Gould returned to live with his parents in Toronto; his "cage in the woods" was the family cottage on Lake Simcoe. Bernhard's Gould is completely absorbed by music and, unlike Wertheimer or the narrator, never engages in writing. The real Gould wrote constantly, and according to his official biographer, Otto Friedrich, left behind "sheaves of manuscripts" and an assortment of lined notepads containing "ideas, letters, drafts of interviews, revisions of articles, stock-market holdings, medical symptoms, his own temperature," and other nonmusical data. Finally, Gould suffered a stroke while sleeping and died in a hospital a few days later. Bernhard uses poetic license to have his Gould die of a stroke at the piano while playing the *Goldberg Variations*.

Why these distortions? In part Bernhard adapts Gould's actual biography to make it fit his own. *Bernhard*, not the Canadian virtuoso, turned fifty-one the year Gould died; *he* had the lung disease that, ever since he began writing at the sanatorium in Grafenhof, became his "second art" of fashioning unending sentences; *he* broke with his family and moved to an isolated house in the country. But Bernhard also distorts the facts of Gould's life to make him into a monolithic, Zarathustrian *Übermensch* of artistic will and power. Gould represented not only a pinnacle of musical virtuosity but, more important, an uncompromising artistic personality who refused to sacrifice his original talent to the demands of critics or public. It is not just Gould's playing but the fact that he stopped playing, turned his back on the world, that fascinated Bernhard. It didn't matter that this example was partly a myth, or that the actual Gould quite cannily orchestrated his public image and record sales. For Bernhard didn't need Glenn Gould, he needed the "idea of Glenn Gould"— the "thought vehicle" with which he could spin out his own literary variation of Gould playing Bach.

The narrator in *The Loser*, who is never identified by name, also resembles Bernhard in several key respects. The brief account he gives of his academic itinerary near the end of the novel corresponds exactly to the novelist's own study in Vienna and Salzburg, the only difference being that the narrator has a house in Desselbrunn rather than the nearby Ohlsdorf, where Bernhard actually resided. (Incidentally, all the place names in the novel are real and are taken from the region of Upper Austria that Bernhard knew since childhood.) The narrator also admits to a "subjective," "unjust" tendency in describing his friend Wertheimer which is undoubtedly part of Bernhard's own troubled conscience: "I would have again mentioned things that were better left unmentioned, things concerning Wertheimer, and with all the injustice and exaggeration that have become my fate, in a word with the subjectivity I myself have always detested but from which I have never been immune."

But just as Bernhard projects positive elements of his own artistic identity into the portrait of Gould, so he deliberately caricatures himself in that of the narrator, who, like "the loser," is a prisoner of Gould's musical example, abandons his career, and spends his life writing and rewriting his essay *About Glenn Gould*. Unlike Bernhard, already the author of some forty published novels and plays, the narrator has never published any of his work, still has no idea what philosophy is despite having devoted the better part of his life to it, and, now that his two closest friends are dead, seems headed for an early grave. "Now I'm alone," he thinks, "since, to tell the truth, I only had two people in my life who gave it any meaning: Glenn and Wertheimer. Now Glenn and Wertheimer are dead and I have to come to terms with this fact."

Bernhard thus operates according to a logic of inventive schizophrenia, splitting and doubling himself into a series of alter egos that are locked in a life-and-death struggle. The external narrative is in fact a metaphysical drama of the divided self. But there is also a third *doppelgänger*, Wertheimer, "the loser." Though not directly modeled after any actual person, the narrator's friend bears traits of Ludwig Wittgenstein, a figure who implicitly and explicitly informs a good deal of Bernhard's writing since *Correction*. Like the philosopher, Wertheimer comes from a wealthy Jewish family in Vienna, has a close but conflictual relationship with his sister, and writes fragmentary "notes" that in the novel are called *Zettel*—the title Wittgenstein used to refer to some of his late philosophical aphorisms. But Wertheimer, though undoubtedly brilliant, is an ironic caricature of Wittgenstein: an envious, weak artist who is destroyed by Gould's superior talent; a sadist who keeps his sister locked up in a quasi-incestuous relationship; and finally a philosophical failure who burns all his notes before committing a spiteful, embarrassing suicide.

With these three characters in place—all of them drawn subjectively from the lives of Gould, Bernhard, and Wittgenstein—the author of *The Loser* proceeds to narrate the same story he tells in virtually every one of his plays and novels: a story of frustrated ambition and (incestuous) love, suicide, and the generally grotesque absurdity of existence. But if the form is the same, Bernhard's genius consists in his ability to vary the main themes and settings for his work, which function as an analogue to his own writing—Frank Lloyd Wright's architecture in *Correction*, the paintings of Goya and Brueghel in *Old Masters*, Ibsen's *The Wild Duck* in *Woodcutters*. Here it is Bach's *Goldberg Variations*, played by Glenn Gould, that provides as it were the basso continuo for Bernhard's own deliberately droning repetitions and variations. With the monologistic, uninterrupted flow of its sentences, the novel conjures up the image of a singer fighting to sustain his breath to the end of an impossibly long, embellished aria. Or, to use the historical reference behind the novel, the image of an insomniac count listening to Goldberg play Bach's variations over and over again. And everywhere we sense Gould's dedication to this music, a dedication so fanatical and inhuman that it extinguishes all personal identity: "My ideal would be, *I would be the Steinway, I wouldn't need Glenn Gould*, he said, I could, by being the Steinway, make Glenn Gould totally superfluous. . . . To wake up one day *and be Steinway and Glenn in one*, he said, I thought, *Glenn Steinway, Steinway Glenn, all for Bach*."

But the analogy goes further. For it is not just Bach's music that informs *The Loser*, but a modernist reading of Baroque music—Bach filtered through the aggressively atonal, mathematical formalism of Schönberg and Webern, whom Bernhard and Gould both admired. This is not the place to detail the considerable similarities between Gould's musical views and Bernhard's prose style. Suffice it to say that both artists appreciated the fugal nature of Baroque music, which mixes without dissolving the differences between two, three, and even four distinct voices. Gould's uncanny ability to sustain the separation between voices in a musical composition bears a striking affinity to Bernhard's narrative schizophrenia. Not surprisingly, both men were fascinated by the problem of impersonation, quotation, and artistic doublings. They also shared a dislike for individualist art forms (like a Mozart sonata or a Balzac novel) based on progression, climax, and reconciliation.

Gould felt that "a sense of discomfort, of unease, could be the sagest of counselors for both artist and audience"; Bernhard enjoyed "shaking people up." Finally, art was for both of them not an end in itself but a way of achieving an ascetic renunciation of the world. "Art should be given the chance to phase itself out," Gould maintained in his self-interview, just as the artist himself should have the necessary inner mobility and strength "to opt creatively out of the human situation." In his acceptance speech for the Austrian State Prize for Literature, Bernhard offered his public the Baroque wisdom that "everything is ridiculous if one thinks of death."

In the final analysis, what matters is that in the *idea* of Glenn Gould Bernhard found something he could love and respect unconditionally, a touchstone with which to judge the world around him. "Those are terrible people," the Jewish professor says to his housekeeper in *Heldenplatz*, "who don't like Glenn Gould. . . . I will have nothing to do with such people, they are dangerous people. . . . I also demand that my wife love Glenn Gould, in that respect I'm a fanatic." To be sure, Gould is the hammer which Bernhard used to unsettle Austria's complacent image of itself as the most musical nation of Europe, the birthplace of Mozart and Schubert. And the "fanatics" who love Gould as much as the narrator does in *The Loser* are also ironic figures, emblems of the absurd limits to which people drive themselves in the name of art. But in Gould Bernhard found a balancing force to the vitriolic satire he couldn't help directing at his fellow Austrians, "with the subjectivity I personally have always detested but from which I have never been immune." This saves *The Loser* from being merely an exercise in verbal wit, caricature, and (self-) mockery. Here we have Bach's music, Gould's artistic dedication, and finally the narrator's confession of love and friendship for the two people who meant everything to him and now are gone. Neither Bernhard nor his narrator is prone to sentimentality—but beneath all their ironic laughter, that confession can still be heard.

MARK M. ANDERSON

Ernst Aichinger at the Austrian Cultural Institute in New York generously provided information for the present remarks; may he and his colleagues be thanked here. M.A.

From

THOMAS
BERNHARD

Frost

A NOVEL

Thomas Bernhard's debut novel, published in German in 1963, and now in English for the first time. Visceral, raw, singular, and distinctive, *Frost* is the story of a friendship between a young man at the beginning of his medical career and a painter who is entering his final days.

Available October 2006, in hardcover from Knopf

$25.95 · 1-4000-4066-3

PLEASE VISIT WWW.AAKNOPF.COM

ALSO BY THOMAS BERNHARD

"The feeling grows that Thomas Bernhard is the most original, concentrated novelist writing in German. His connections . . . with the great constellation of Kafka, Musil, and Broch become ever clearer." —George Steiner, The Times Literary Supplement

GARGOYLES

Gargoyles, one of Bernhard's earliest novels, is a singular, surreal study of the nature of humanity. One morning a doctor and his son set out on daily rounds through the grim, mountainous Austrian countryside. They observe the colorful characters they encounter—from an innkeeper whose wife has been murdered to a crippled musical prodigy kept in a cage—coping with physical misery, madness, and the brutality of the austere landscape. The parade of human grotesques culminates in a hundred-page monologue by an eccentric, paranoid prince, a relentlessly flowing cascade of words that is classic Bernhard.

Fiction/Literature/1-4000-7755-9

VINTAGE INTERNATIONAL
Available at your local bookstore, or call toll-free to order:
1-800-793-2665 (credit cards only).